Praise for V
Rocky Mou

"Vivian Arend pours intense passion into her novels, and *Rocky Mountain Heat* is no exception."

~ *Library Journal*

"Plenty of surprisingly sexy and emotionally tender moments line the story and will have your attention rapt all the way to the end. I am eager to see where these wild ranch boys take us next and the very brave, but extremely lucky women who get to tame them."

~ *Long and Short Reviews*

"If you love books about smokin' hot cowboys and their families you must try Six Pack Ranch... This book is on my keeper and re-read shelves."

~ *Guilty Pleasure Book Reviews*

"*Rocky Mountain Heat* is a wonderfully romantic and sexy story...This is my first Vivian Arend read and it will not be my last. I'll be picking up *Rocky Mountain Haven* ASAP! I must know what those sexy Coleman brothers are up to next."

~ *FictionVixen*

Look for these titles by
Vivian Arend

Now Available:

Rocky Mountain Heat

Vivian Arend

SAMHAIN
PUBLISHING

Samhain Publishing, Ltd.
11821 Mason Montgomery Road, 4B
Cincinnati, OH 45249
www.samhainpublishing.com

Rocky Mountain Heat
Copyright © 2012 by Vivian Arend
Print ISBN: 978-1-60928-799-3
Digital ISBN: 978-1-60928-551-7

Editing by Anne Scott
Cover by Angela Waters

This book has been previously published and has been revised and expanded from its original release.

First Samhain Publishing, Ltd. electronic publication: November 2011
First Samhain Publishing, Ltd. print publication: October 2012

Dedication

For all the men and women I know who work the land and love the country. Small towns and gravel roads, wire fences and work that never ends. It's worth it.

Prologue

"Are you sure you can't last a bit longer?" Travis looked away, but not before she'd spotted the disappointment in his eyes. The annoyance.

Jaxi leaned her temple against the wooden boards of the pen, fighting to keep herself vertical. The familiar scent of farm animals did nothing to ease the swirling pain. She felt like the bottom of a horse stall and faking her way through any more of the day was impossible. "I'm sorry. I have to go home now," she pleaded.

"We bought tickets for the grandstand show tonight and—"

"Why are you two still here? I thought you'd headed back to the fairgrounds. All our livestock showings are done." Blake Coleman's deep voice cut through the pounding to soothe her aching head. She opened her eyes a crack to peer up at him.

People wandered past, admiring the animals on display in the livestock pavilion of the Stampede grounds. Watching the rodeo and chuck-wagon races kept many of the visitors entertained, but a good crowd remained here in the quiet of the barns, far away from the roar of the midway rides. A low murmur of voices and the contented sounds of animals filled the oversized building. All of that faded into the background as she focused on Blake's strong jaw and concerned gaze.

"Ahhh, Jaxi's being a wuss and wants to cut out early," Travis bitched.

"Jaxi? A wuss? Get real." Blake tugged her arm to bring her to his side. His hand rose to her forehead and she caught her breath.

In spite of the lingering sensation of being kicked by a mule, his touch had its usual effect. The tingling in her limbs had nothing to do with the fever consuming her. She dropped her gaze and bit her lip. He wasn't supposed to affect her this way. Going out with Travis put big brother Blake firmly off limits.

"Damn, you're burning hot. Jaxi, why didn't you mention you weren't feeling well? You guys could have done the Stampede another time. Last day isn't until Sunday." A crease folded between his eyes.

"Travis wanted to come today and so did his buddies. I was fine until after lunch. I guess I should have stayed home." Jaxi wrapped her arms tighter to contain the shivers that threatened to surface. She drew farther from Blake's body and the temptation to lean into him, let him hold her close.

"Travis will take you home in my truck and I'll drive the others later," Blake offered.

"I want to stay for the show. All my friends are here and I don't want to leave..." Travis's voice trailed off. Blake had slipped him a head nod, indicating he wanted a private conversation.

Jaxi sat on a nearby bale of hay, holding as motionless as possible in the hopes the world would stop spinning. Their voices went quiet but remained clear even as Blake dragged Travis away from her down the length of the main barn of the exhibition grounds.

"She's your girlfriend and she's sick. I'd think you'd want to get her home safely instead of taking off to hang with your friends. Come on, Travis, do the right thing for a frickin' change."

"Hell, Blake, it's just...this is the first time in a long while some of my buds have made the Stampede."

"Not good enough. Any better reason to leave her high and dry?"

"Fuck you." There was a pause, then she barely heard the rest. Travis dropped his volume to a whisper. "Things ain't been so hot with Jaxi lately and, well, I planned on breaking up with her sometime soon. So it would be a damn pain in the ass to leave when everyone else is sticking around having a good time. I'll just go home alone and end up with blue balls again anyway."

Jaxi bit her lip. So, the other shoe dropped. Travis had reached his limit of her not *putting out* for him, even though she'd willingly played his games.

The room whirled.

Oh hell, she needed to lie down. She stumbled to the nearest empty stall, forced the door open and collapsed onto the clean straw. She closed her eyes but everything kept turning in circles, their voices echoing strangely in her ears.

"Shit, she's messed up my whole evening." Travis's whine broke off suddenly, followed by a solid thump, as if something hit the ground. "What the fuck was that for, you asshole?"

Blake's contempt was thick enough to cut. "I shoved you because if I slugged you Ma would give me hell. At least until I explained why, and I don't want to have that conversation with her. Damn it, Jaxi's sick and you're bitching about not getting any? You're an ass. I'll bring her with me. I have to get some of the stock out of here anyway. You drive the old pickup back after the show. There's room for everyone who came with us to town. But, Travis, I'm warning you. You're the designated driver. You drink more than one beer between now and getting home, and I'll take you apart for being an overall idiot as well as a shit to Jaxi."

Their voices died away. She lay still, waiting for something to happen. Soft footsteps approached. The door of the stall swung open and Jaxi swayed as she sat up. Blake stared from his six-foot-plus height. The anger tingeing his face faded as he shook his head sorrowfully and held a hand to her.

"Ah hell, Slick. You're a strong one, aren't you? In spite of Travis giving you grief. Come on, let's get you home."

As he lifted her to her feet and wrapped an arm around her shoulders, gratitude and a whole lot of other emotions rippled through her. She was glad she wasn't the one who'd pissed him off. Glad that he'd care for her, just like always.

She stumbled and he caught her, guiding her shaky steps out of the barn. Even with her mind cluttered with fever, she recognized the irony—here she was in his arms the way she'd always dreamed of, and the situation was the furthest thing from what she truly wanted.

Sometimes life sucked.

It took far too long to hitch the trailer and load the animals headed back to the ranch. Blake checked Jaxi a couple of times. She did nothing more than lift a finger to indicate she was still alive—although looking thoroughly miserable—as she waited in the cab of the truck. Thank God, she didn't seem nauseous, only dizzy. Blake shoveled down a quick sandwich as he forced the rear doors shut. He wasn't about to eat in front of her, just in case, but it had been a long time since he'd eaten and they had a good two and a half hour drive to get home.

He opened the door to find her asleep on the bench seat. She'd hauled an old blanket from behind the backrest and wrapped the threadbare material around herself, but even the extra layer hadn't stopped the shaking.

"Slick, what have you done to yourself this time?"

Blake lifted her slightly and managed to get behind the wheel, arranging her to rest in his lap. She muttered something before shivering from head to toe. He got them on the highway headed north out of town before turning his attention downward.

She'd braided her blonde hair into two pigtails. The style made her look closer to twelve than eighteen. At twelve she'd still been Jax, her best friends his youngest brothers, the twins Joel and Jesse. He could see the three of them in his head, running wild through the horse stable, and building castles in the bales crowding the hayloft of the Colemans' ranch. An only child, Jaxi came calling on a regular basis, longing for company. Whenever her ma and daddy got busy, she would cross the field between their properties and jump wholeheartedly into whatever mischief the Colemans were cooking up.

At fourteen she'd declared they all had to call her Jaxi, and that's when the trouble started. All of a sudden she wasn't only a great fishing and riding buddy to the boys, there were hips and breasts and all the interesting parts that went along with being a girl.

Blake pushed a loose strand of hair from her face. Her forehead was burning hot under his fingers, and shivers continued to rack her body. Her slim form fit on the seat with difficulty because of her long legs, even with them curled up tight as she lay in his lap.

And wasn't that the most damning part of it all. Here she was in his lap, exactly where he'd longed to have her, and exactly where he had no right to want her. Twenty-eight years was old enough to know better.

But young enough, it appeared, to still be a stupid ass.

Even burning with fever she was incredibly beautiful. He fought the attraction he felt, feeling dirty for thinking about her that way. Ten years between them. For heaven's sake, he'd been the one to hold the reins the first time she rode a horse. He'd carried her home another day when she'd fallen off and gotten the wind knocked out of her. He'd become family to the lonely little girl, and he had no right to admire her changing body, her bright eyes or her quick wit.

And his fool of a brother planned on breaking up with her? At nineteen Travis thought he was God's gift to women, but at times like this Blake wondered if Travis was one shovel short of a full load.

Why was Jaxi going out with the ass in the first place? Why not one of the twins, even if they were a year younger than her? Hell, why not Daniel? Of the six brothers on the ranch, did she have to pick the one with the biggest ego and the least brains?

Blake took the off-ramp and got onto the secondary highway leading to the town of Rocky Mountain House. The small town near their homes lay nestled in the rolling foothills up against the towering Alberta Rockies. At this time of day the roads were empty—everyone headed to the city already long gone. His was the only vehicle around, and behind him dust rose to the bright blue sky like a trail of gunpowder toward the barrel.

He was in so much trouble when it came to this sweet girl, and from what he knew she still was sweet, in spite of his asshole of a brother's attempts to change the situation.

He'd overheard them a few weeks ago...

He paused two steps inside the barn doors to give his eyes a chance to adjust from the blinding June sunshine. Moans and other suspicious noises led him back to the tack room. It didn't take a genius to figure out who it was and what was happening on the other side of the closed door. From the sound of it, things were getting hot and heavy. Blake didn't deliberately step closer to eavesdrop.

Hell, yes, he did. He didn't trust Travis as far as he could throw him.

The kissing and the rustling built his curiosity to a peak before Jaxi muttered, "Uh-uh, cool it," and someone knocked something over.

"Oh, damn, Jaxi, you're killing me here. I need you. I really need you, baby."

Blake's lips twisted into a grin at her unladylike response—a loud snort.

"I'm not stupid, Travis. You won't die if we don't have sex. Get over it already. I'm not willing—"

"You don't love me."

"Damn right, I don't. You don't love me either. We're friends, that's all."

You tell him, girl. Blake snuck to the far end of the hall where he would remain safely hidden even if one of them decided to bust out of the room without warning. He didn't feel a lick of guilt for listening in. The only self-reproach was over the way his gut tensed, imagining having Jaxi in his own arms to kiss and caress.

He beat down the impulse and listened harder.

"Jaxi, you know you like it when I touch you. I get your motor running. It's just another thing I can do to make you feel good. Make us both feel real good. Come on, sweetheart, it'll be special."

"In a barn? Travis Coleman, you may be considered the hottest thing around by the rest of the girls in town, but you need a little work on your romancing."

The sound of creaking floorboards warned Blake to fade into the corner more.

"Don't leave me hurting here, sweetheart. Come on back and help me out. You know I like it when you touch me."

The door squeaked as she shoved it open. "Travis, I was enjoying myself, but when you push the boundaries every time we fool around, it kills the mood. I've told you I'm not having sex. Not with you or anyone until I'm older, no matter what kinky games you like to play. It's something special and I want to save it."

"Yeah, I remember."

"Then why do you keep trying to convince me to go further than I want?"

"Because I... Oh hell, are you going to help me here or what?"

The door slammed and Jaxi's strong voice rang out. "Talk to the hand, Travis, talk to the hand."

Blake had waited in the shadows until Travis, cussing a fair bit, hauled his ass back to the house. While he'd been proud of Jaxi for sticking to her guns, that episode had

16

probably been another step in the beginning of the end for the two of them.

He looked at her again, lying in his lap so innocently. He was such a bastard. Even while he wanted to break his brother's head for trying to seduce her, he had to stop himself from stroking her cheek to see if her skin was as soft as it looked.

She moaned, and her limbs jerked, arms flailing. She struck the dash with one hand, the wheel with the other.

"Whoa, take it easy." He laid a restraining touch on her shoulder.

"Travis?"

"No, Slick, it's Blake. Remember?"

Jaxi rolled over to stare at him. Her eyes were glazed, and she seemed to focus on something beyond him. Only a second later her face flushed and flared to anger.

"Damn it, Travis, I told you I wouldn't give you head while you drive. Pull over right now."

Holy shit! What the hell had his brother been doing with this girl? "I'm not Travis... You've got to listen, hon—"

"Pull the truck over now, you son of a bitch." She forced herself to a sitting position, body weaving from side to side. "I swear you're going to be the death of me. Stop this truck now or I'll tell him."

Tell who? Tell what?

She yelled louder, smacking her fists against his arm. The blows weren't hard enough to cause much pain but with her off-kilter balance and the rough road, she kept knocking herself around. Blake grabbed her with one hand, pinning her arms in place as he steered the truck and trailer off to the side as quickly as possible.

"You've got to relax. I'm not Travis, I'm Blake. Ah, damn it, Slick, you are one sick little girl."

"Yeah, well, you're pretty sick yourself. You want to break up with me but you want one final farewell, is that it? Fine by me."

A jolt of panic struck. She must have heard Travis back at the fairgrounds. Now what should he do? Try to calm her or let Travis drown in the hole he'd dug for himself?

She threw her leg across him as if she were jumping a calf in the roping contest.

"This is it. You hear me? As of tomorrow we're not a couple anymore and you can go fuck whoever you want without me around as a decoy. I've had enough of the pretending." While she spoke, she slipped loose the buckle on his belt in one smooth motion.

Blake jerked. He scrambled for her hands, trying to catch her, trying to stop her as she dragged at his zipper.

It only took a moment before he held her wrists immobile, her strong body protesting his control as she cussed and writhed in his lap. Her hot breath fell across his cheek as she leaned against him. Suddenly, all her tension slipped away and she melted in his arms. One breast nudged his chest as she tilted her body to the side. Their hands remained trapped between their torsos, and yet she attempted to snuggle closer. Her violent shouts gave way to little moans. Her tongue slipped along his sweating neck, a satisfied noise escaping.

She may have lost her stiffness, but he'd found every single bit of it. His shoulders tensed, his abdomen muscles went taut, but it was his damn cock that betrayed him the most. Against his will, his erection rose to meet her. Harder than granite in less than five seconds—from the moment her hands brushed the front of his groin.

He wasn't getting excited because it was Jaxi. Simply because there was a female touching him. That's what he tried to tell himself. No, it was strictly an automatic male reaction. It wasn't because this was Jaxi and Blake had dreamed of this for longer than he wanted to admit.

He wasn't the kind of asshole to sit and let his brother's feverish, soon-to-be-ex-girlfriend fondle him at the side of the road. He wasn't such a jerk he'd actually try to justify keeping her nestled tight to him for a couple more seconds because it was the best thing he'd ever felt in his life, her hands pressed innocently against the ridge of his now fully engorged cock.

About then he realized he didn't quite know how to deal with the situation once he did stop her. What if he spoke? Having her suddenly clue in he wasn't Travis like she imagined—what kind of shock would that be? She'd be so damn embarrassed.

"So cold." Another shiver rocked her and he instinctively cradled her. "Warm me up."

He didn't need to be any warmer. He was going to burn in hell forever for this. Her lips touched his neck again, and he attempted to twist out of reach. Impossible. They were trapped between the back of the bench and the steering wheel. With a little more room to manoeuvre, he could open the door and get them both out. Hopefully the cooler air outside the cab would bring her back to her senses. He reached around her to disengage the wheel lock. Jaxi wiggled, moving over him with a killing touch, slipping her palms against his chest as her hips settled tight over his groin and the erection he shouldn't have.

He was a bastard. The split second he paused, savouring the sensations rippling through his body, turned his self-loathing to high. He forced himself to continue to swing the wheel away. Finally with enough room, Blake leaned forward and reached for the door release.

He was yanked to a stop as Jaxi buried her hands in his hair and bit his neck, slowly undulating her heated crotch over his aching cock. Blake wrapped his right arm around her and pinned her in place, ignoring the way his balls throbbed with need.

How this innocent trip home had digressed from uncomfortable to totally fucked up he had no idea. Forget going to hell, he was already there, being tormented by Satan himself as the old boy directed the little fever-induced drama happening on the side of the 761 Secondary Highway.

A quick glance to be sure no cars were in the immediate area was all he spared before shoving his foot hard at the door as he yanked the release handle. The frame swung open in a rush, recoiling to hang in the line of traffic.

A cooling breeze struck his sweated brow the same moment Jaxi sucked his skin. Blake bit back a groan and twisted them both, his legs absorbing the impact as he cradled her close and escaped the confining quarters of the cab.

She tucked her heated forehead into the crook of his neck, right where she'd been sucking on him only a second before. Another shiver took her, and he turned his back to the wind to provide protection.

"So thirsty." Jaxi lifted her face, and he examined her flushed cheeks. She licked her lips, her eyes half-closed with heavy lids. Her head lolled back slightly, and he raced to deposit her on the bench seat and find her a drink. Her hands shook as she tilted the water bottle, and he reached to help her before she sloshed the contents all over.

When she crawled away from him to the passenger side of the truck, wrapped the blanket around her shoulders and settled her cheek on the seat, he was tempted to dump the remaining liquid in the plastic bottle over his head to cool his own raging fever.

Blake leaned on the side door and adjusted his dick, willing the damn thing to admit defeat and retreat. That hadn't been too bad. Behind him, Jaxi moaned and his cock jerked. No, not too bad at all if he was a masochist. His only hope lay in her feverish confusion to last long enough she thought he was Travis. As long as she didn't talk to Travis in the next while about trying to ride him like a pony on the trip home.

Oh hell, he might as well face it. He was dead.

Blake crawled into the cab, wincing a little at the tight confinement of his jeans. Jaxi wiggled closer, resting her head back on his thigh, the tangled strands of her loose blonde hair covering his crotch. He brushed the wisps away carefully in the hopes she wouldn't wake from her stupor.

"Oh, Slick, what a mess."

He glanced up and adjusted the rearview mirror that had gotten bumped during their tangled encounter. A bright red mark on his neck caught his eye, and he groaned in frustration. Like he was going to be able to explain that one easily. He shook his head and aimed the truck for home. In his lap, Jaxi's feverish cheek burned a hole into his thigh while his unanswerable lust burned a hole in his conscience.

Chapter One

"I'm fine, boys, stop your fussing." Marion Coleman shook her good hand at the twins as they hovered nearby. "I didn't need the wheelchair. It's a silly hospital policy." She shot to her feet, batting Jesse and Joel away.

Blake offered his help, and she smiled, the edges of her mouth remaining tight and the lines at the corner of her eyes deep. She might make light of the situation but it was clear her arm hurt. A lot. She tucked her fingers around his elbow and dragged him across the hospital parking lot, her rapid pace unhampered by the heavy cast covering her right arm from wrist to shoulder.

They stopped beside one of the huge crew-cab ranch trucks, the twins scrambling into the backseat. Marion stared in disgust at the hand pull she couldn't reach.

"Why did you boys all have to grow to over six feet? None of you own a nice little Jetta or Mustang for me to be able to slide into. Just these monster trucks. I have to use a ladder to reach the seat."

"You fed us too well." Blake worked at remaining gentle as he lifted her to the bench, careful not to jar her arm. He'd closed the door and stepped around to the driver's side before he realized it was impossible for her to buckle her seat belt with the cast in the way. He slid behind the wheel and reached to help her. "Let me get it, Ma. You're going to find things a bit awkward for a spell."

"I hate this." Marion stared past him out the window, a touch of fury in her eyes.

"Maybe you should have waited for help picking the apples," Joel piped up from the backseat.

"She did ask, you jerk, remember?" Jesse said. "First we had to finish the back field before the weekend, then Dad asked us to—"

"This is no one's fault. You boys are all busy, with the hay ready to be cut and the animals to care for. I wanted to get the apples before you had time to help me and, well, I've never fallen out of a tree before in my life. Been climbing that one for years." His mom wiggled around in her seat to shake a finger at her youngest sons. "It was an accident. I don't blame either of you, so don't you think you did something wrong. But now I'm going to need some help. Not only do I have a bushel of apples to deal with, there's the garden that needs to be put up, laundry for the family and the cookin' and..." She returned her gaze to the window. "I've caused a mess, boys, and that's the plain truth."

Blake touched her hand softly. His ma was a hard-working woman and not just at the ranch. She'd toiled beside his father for over thirty years, doing everything inside the house, plus caring for and raising six boys, gardening and dealing with the livestock. In addition to her chores at home, she'd always been there for the community, for newcomers and new babies, and whenever a person needed a helping hand.

Having a broken arm was going to bother her a lot—the pain of it mending, and the annoyance of everything she'd be unable to do for a while. Sitting and watching others work was not her style.

"Well, I guess it's time the neighbours get a chance to show a little lovin' your way and come to give you a hand." Blake hoped she'd actually allow people to step forward.

"Blake Coleman, I've never done anything in my life in the hopes to be repaid."

He backpedaled. "That's not what I meant. We know you do things because you want to help others, Ma, but you've got to accept the friends who come to chip in. I'll do what I can—we all will. Even though we're temporarily back under your roof doesn't mean you have to feed us and tend to our needs. It's not as if we haven't all cared for ourselves before. We're big boys. In fact, you need to let us know what we have to take over for you."

Marion shook her head. "You say you want to help, but when are you going to manage that right now? The fall is the busiest time of year between the animals, the fields and the furniture orders. You can't add my chores to your list. Everyone else in town is just as busy."

She lifted the cast in the air tentatively. "I'll figure out how to work around this. I'll get by."

Blake looked in the rearview mirror and exchanged worried glances with his brothers. Something had to happen. He didn't know who was available, but sooner than later, his ma was right. They were going to need help.

Blake's truck rumbled up the long drive toward the Colemans' ranch house, past the cars in the parking area, right to the head of the circular driveway. News had always traveled fast in small towns, even before the invention of the cell phone.

Jaxi turned from the kitchen window she'd been staring out, grabbed her tray of food and headed quietly into the main living area.

The neighbours and community folk who'd stopped in shifted from the living room onto the front porch to watch Mike Coleman approach like a bull headed for his mate. He'd been in Calgary fetching supplies when Marion had fallen. By the time the boys contacted him, there was no time to get to the hospital. Marion was already in a cast and being brought home.

Mike yanked open the truck door, lifted his wife carefully and carried her to the foot of the stairs, ignoring her loud complaints at his behavior.

"I'll carry you whenever I want, woman. Don't you *ever* scare me like that again." He placed her feet on the ground and held her as close as the awkward cast allowed. One long tender kiss on her forehead followed before he turned her to face the concerned onlookers. "Well, she's still in one piece, folks. I guess she learned to bounce pretty good."

As a few of her friends surrounded Marion to talk, Mike guiding her up the steps, Jaxi slipped away from her perch just inside the door to pour more coffee. She placed a couple of plates piled with cookies and squares on the long family table for people to serve themselves, then snuck back into the kitchen. Mike followed her, a sigh of what sounded suspiciously like relief escaping his lips.

"You're an angel. Thanks for helping on such short notice."

Jaxi grinned. "Mrs. Wade and Mrs. Leaner brought the baking. There are four casseroles in the fridge, and another six in the freezer. If you freeze anything else that arrives—"

"Whoa, girl," Mike interrupted. "I want to talk to you. I chatted with the doctor when he called, and he told me Marion's going to need some assistance for a couple weeks. Around the house and personal like. I'll do what I can, but you've got the training and he recommended you. You have the time to come and help us? It won't require a lot of nursing."

"I'm not a nurse, Mr. Coleman. I do have a first aid certificate."

"And a bit more."

Jaxi nodded. The strange assortment of classes she'd completed at the local college and through correspondence courses over the past couple of years didn't give her a degree. Still, her training had covered many areas. Personal care she could do.

"It's short notice, but Dr. Yale thought you were free."

Jaxi washed her hands in the sink and bent to get a new hand towel from the bottom drawer. "He should know. I've been acting as a nanny for him and Katie, but she's decided to stay home and care for the kids herself. My last day was Friday."

Mike clapped her on the shoulder. "Will you do it? We'll figure out some sort of pay rate for the nursing and such."

She turned to face him, smiling to soften the words. "Please don't talk about paying me. You and Mrs. C have always been there for me, and I'd love to return the favour."

"The thing is, you won't be able to do anything else to earn money. She's going to need you here twenty-four/seven at first. And now that I think of it, there's the garden that needs to be dealt with. I don't want to swindle you. We'll pay. I insist."

Jaxi grabbed another tray from under the sink for the empty plates and cups. "Let's discuss the details later. You go and visit with your neighbours—you know they won't make a lengthy stay. I'm happy to come and help for as long as you need me."

He gave her hand a quick squeeze, then returned to the living room.

Jaxi wandered the main floor, cleaning up and making more coffee. She figured out which of the casseroles to pop in the oven for supper, peeking in the fridge to see what else to feed the horde of hungry men who would descend on the house in a few hours.

Marion's accident had come at an awkward time, with more bodies than usual living under the Coleman roof. Jaxi had wondered when she'd heard Mike had rented out the second family home to a needy newcomer to the community a few weeks ago. The three oldest—Blake, Daniel and Matt—had been living in the nearby house for years. While the twins would return to college dorms in a few weeks, the rest of them, including her ex-boyfriend Travis, worked the Coleman spread with their father. Having all six boys crowded back into their childhood home made for a bizarre flashback—and a lot more work than Marion would be able to keep up with one-handed.

Jaxi finished her tidying and moved to peel the mess of potatoes she'd found soaking in the pantry sink. If she was honest, at least with herself, offering to ease the load for Mrs. Coleman was only part of the reason she'd come over today. The other? It was finally time to make her play. She wanted Blake, and she was ready to do anything to get him to see her as more than the little girl next door.

Others in her high school seemed overly eager to move to Calgary or Edmonton immediately after graduation, desperate to get away from the small town. The ones who returned to visit joked about the lack of culture, the lack of atmosphere, and the lack of *everything* in Rocky Mountain House. She thought many times it wasn't the location that was screwed up, but their attitudes.

She looked through the window of the rambling house toward the rolling foothills and the high Rockies rising beyond them. The Coleman ranch was set in one of the most beautiful areas in the whole world, yet young people were scrambling over each other to get away.

She knew better. There was nowhere she'd rather be than here.

A warm spot hit her, right in the middle of her chest. It wasn't just the location that made her happy. There was no one she'd rather be with than Blake Coleman. She'd do anything to have him be the one holding her tight. To care for the land at his side. It'd been that way forever. Every time she looked at him, pictured him—heck, dreamed of him—it was enough to get her juices flowing. The man was a hunk of handsome, generous to a fault and smooth in all the right ways.

Jaxi smiled as she dropped the diced potatoes into a pot and swirled cold water over them. She was finally grown up enough there would be less complaining among the gossipmongers. All she'd wanted her whole life was to be a rancher's wife. Blake's wife.

Staying here put her in a great position to let him know how things would go down from now on. He'd been looking ragged around the edges the past couple times she'd seen him in town. He needed a little caring for.

She was more than up for the calling.

"Jaxi? Wow, girl. Mike just told me you planned on lending us a hand for a bit but I never expected you'd..." Marion leaned on the doorframe to the kitchen, the clumsy bulk of her arm held cautiously in front of her. The older woman grinned and the expression took years off her face. "Well, actually, yes, I did expect you to jump in and make yourself at home. Your momma going to miss you if you bunk here with us?"

"No, ma'am. I've been living at the Yales' place since the spring so she's fine with the occasional visit. I'm all yours," Jaxi said.

"Good. We'll have to see about where to tuck you. The upstairs bedrooms are all full with the twins still here for another few weeks. We can put you in the guest cabin or in the den downstairs, or move one of the other boys from their room in the basement. The cabin is the most private."

"It's also a lot farther away if you need me quick. I really don't mind the den."

Marion sniffed. "I can get Daniel or Blake to move."

Jaxi shook a hand at her. "Please don't do that. I don't need much space for my stuff." Jaxi popped the potatoes on the stove and set the heat to boil. "For supper, there's a green bean casserole from the Thiessens and a large pot of stew from the Laings. You got salad fixings in the garden?"

"Some. I'll go—"

"You'll do no such thing. How are you going to pick cucumbers and lettuce with one hand? I can get everything in the oven and warming in five minutes. You stay and watch the potatoes don't boil over." Jaxi pulled herself up sharp before turning a guilty smile on the other woman. "Not that I plan on bossing you around in your own kitchen or anything."

Marion laughed out loud. "Oh, Jaxi, it's good to have you here." She tugged Jaxi in close for a hug, pressing a kiss to her cheek. "You go right ahead and boss all you want. I'll warn you if you step over the line. I consider you a part of this family, you know that, don't you?"

Jaxi glided around, prepping things for supper. She grabbed the garden pail and hurried through the back door. From Marion's lips to God's ears.

Blake finished up early in the shop. He'd seen the neighbours' cars trickle away and figured he should head in to help with supper preparations. His dad was all right in the kitchen, but unless they wanted to live on pancakes for the next few weeks all of them would need to pull a little extra duty.

He marched around to the back of the house and the lower entrance. When his great-grandpa built the ranch house, he'd included enough room for all six of his boys and a few extra hired hands. They had worked the land by hand and with horses, time-consuming and backbreaking labour raising cattle and tending fields. In those days the bunkhouse attached to the house by an open walkway, but years ago the family had closed the path in and turned the extra space into a shower room and private entrance for the boys to access their downstairs bedrooms. Even though the ranch was now fully modernized, it was still dirty and exhausting work.

He unbuttoned his shirt, stripped the soiled fabric from his body and wiped the sweat from his neck. It was hot for late August, and he hadn't even been in the tractor with the broken air conditioning. Daniel had drawn the short straw this morning.

Blake headed to the outdoor shower. It was safe, as all the visiting vehicles were gone, and he much preferred to wash up in the open air while it was this warm. He stripped off his jeans and boots, pitching the clothes into a pile. He threw his boots on the rack inside and grabbed a towel from the shelf over the door before returning to the bright afternoon sunshine and blasting the water on. Joel, the music addict in the family, had wired speakers on either side of the outdoor area. With a flick of a switch, a country station blared about hurtin' and lovin' and leavin'. Blake smiled as he lathered up and sang along with Randy Travis.

30

Daniel and Matt sauntered by, enormous grins splitting their faces.

"What's your problem? Either of you want the shower? I'm just 'bout done."

Matt ignored the question, but he snickered before entering the house. Daniel shook his head. "I'll use the ones inside. You're a brave man, Blake, braver than I thought."

Blake turned off the water and toweled himself vigorously. "What the hell is the matter with you? Tractor heat-fry your brains?"

"Let's say I like my privacy more than you. Is Mama all right?" Daniel asked.

"Cast the size of a lamb on her arm. We're going to have to pick up the slack over the next while. It'll be tough for her to get any work done."

"Oh, she'll be fine, Blake. I'm pretty sure she'll have the help she needs. Now, you've got me curious. You plan on joining us at the supper table dressed that way or a little more formal?" Daniel grinned again as he turned to stare out into the yard.

Blake stepped next to him, towel held in a fist at his hip. He followed Daniel's gaze. He looked past the walkway, the garden and the greenhouse, clear to the sheep and cattle barns without seeing anything unusual. Shaking his head he retreated toward the house. "I swear, you get harder and harder to understand. Of course I'm dressing. You think I plan on prancing around stark naked in front of everybody?"

Idiot.

He scooped up his dirty clothes, stopping to deposit them in the laundry room. The piles waiting on the floor only took a minute to deal with. Blake loaded the oversized washer and got it going. He ducked into his bedroom to pull on clean jeans and a T-shirt, wondering how long he'd be able to keep up with the washing before his ma found out and tried to take over.

Walking the familiar path through the sleeping area of the basement, striding past TV and recreation rooms toward the stairs to the main level—even after living elsewhere for years, the place felt like home.

Appetizing scents greeted him as he stepped onto the landing—rich beef stew, mashed potatoes and something that smelled like apple pie. The neighbours, it had to be. Damn it was good to live in an area where people took care of each other. Maybe his father's dreaded pancakes could be avoided for a few days.

Blake rounded the corner to see his folks resting easy in the family room, talking together quietly. In the adjoining dining area, the massive table that could comfortably sit a dozen was already set for the meal with pickles and salads, butter and sliced bread.

"Wow, ladies help organize supper before they left?" Blake asked as he settled on the couch across from his father. "Looks great. We've got a wonderful bunch of friends, don't we?"

Marion nodded. "Well, yes, we do, Blake, but actually it was—"

"You get that furniture order ready today, Blake?" Mike interrupted. His parents exchanged peculiar glances. "I know you had to take a break to help your ma. If you need a hand after supper, the boys and I can come and load the last of it."

Blake sat back in his chair. "I'd appreciate that. There's still a couple of items to haul together, but it won't take long." The strange looks continued. "Did they give you some happy gas while you were in the hospital today, Ma? Or is it a full moon tonight? Everyone is acting bewitched."

She smiled innocently and raised her eyebrows. "I don't know what you mean. I believe supper is ready, so ring the bell, please?"

Blake strode to the side of the room and picked up the hammer for the dinner bell. They used an old-fashioned triangle to call for meals, and in spite of being a grown man, he still loved to chime the meal in. One place that his past memories of family time blended into his future.

Or maybe it was a simply Pavlovian reflex—ring the bell and salivating could begin.

Soon the table groaned with food. He never would have guessed his ma had a broken arm by the way the food overflowed the bowls. He and his dad transferred dish after dish from the sideboard until his mouth watered. There were three salads, a huge bowl of corn on the cob slathered with butter, mashed potatoes, the stew, a couple of different casseroles and the biggest apple cobbler he'd ever seen in his life.

Blake shifted around to access his usual spot, waiting while his dad seated his ma. Her expression as she picked up her fork in her left hand was priceless—another tough challenge she had to face. The rest of the boys filtered in, all scrubbed and tidy, a vast improvement from the sweaty mess he'd seen less than thirty minutes earlier. Jesse wore a collared shirt, and Blake raised a brow in his direction.

"Hot date tonight, stud?"

"Just looking presentable for the family." Jesse ignored his brothers' laughter and grabbed a chair opposite Matt.

Joel wandered from the kitchen carrying a couple of pitchers. He held the door open with his hip and spoke to someone behind him. Blake did a fast check. Why was there an extra place set at the table?

His question was answered soon enough as Jaxi floated through the door carrying the gravy boat. She chuckled at something Joel said before depositing the dish and taking her seat in the only empty chair. The one directly across from him.

Blake's mouth went dry and a loud roar of blood in his ears deafened him. Shit, he was in a mess of trouble.

Chapter Two

Jaxi was so busy passing food bowls she missed his question. Jesse nudged her in the ribs, and she turned to discover Blake's storm-grey eyes staring at her. Jesse's fingers lingered on her side, and she pinched his wrist to prompt him to withdraw them.

Jesse was fun, but Blake...he made her body ache.

"Are you still working for the doctor and his wife?" Blake asked again.

Mike cleared his throat. "Actually, Jaxi's got a new job." All heads swung toward the end of the table.

"She'll be my helper for the next bit." Marion made a face at her arm before glancing up and putting on what Jaxi was coming to recognize as her make-the-best-of-it expression— something midway between a grimace and a grin. "Doctor's orders are that I have a nursemaid, and if I have to have one, she's my first choice."

Joel leaned over and whispered as he scooped another spoonful of stew onto her plate. "You'd be my first choice as well. Wanna play *doctor* with me later?"

Jaxi hid her laugh behind a cough. She had to cool the twins off and fast if her plan to catch Blake's attention was going to work. She looked across to see Blake's eyes darken as his gaze flicked between her and where Joel's elbow rested on her chair.

Interesting. A tiny flicker of feminine intuition trembled with hope.

Marion told Daniel about the compound fracture of her arm and how long the cast needed to stay on and all the details he'd missed while trapped in the tractor hauling bales. Jaxi enjoyed her supper, taking time to lick every drop of the savoury stew from her fork, listening to the easy conversation about what needed to be accomplished in the fields the following day and what animals had to be transferred where.

She watched each of the faces around her in turn to see what their reaction was to the announcement she would be in their hair for the next while. Travis gave her his usual smoldering stare, the one that made her wonder if he was still attracted to her, in spite of everything else that had gone south between them. Daniel and Matt seemed pleased to have her around, in their typical non-threatening and non-sexual way. The twins—well, they were a little too delighted by her presence, but she'd already suspected she'd have to nip any plans of theirs in the bud.

"Pass the potatoes," Matt said, scooping the last of the sliced cucumbers onto his plate.

"Sorry, Daniel finished them."

Jaxi pushed back her chair. "There's still more in the kitchen, I'll go—"

"You sit. I'll get them. Everything is delicious but you've barely eaten anything." Jesse held her in place as he grabbed one of the empty bowls and trotted away.

Jaxi sat comfortably and looked around. A feeling of contentment rose at being here with the family, accepted and cared for by all of them. She checked Marion with a casual glance. The woman was managing all right for her first meal with her left hand, although she seemed to be running out of steam.

Mike was doing a little examining of his own. "Young lady, you make sure to eat enough. You'll be working hard the next couple of weeks and we don't want you to overdo it."

Jaxi pulled a face at him. "Jesse exaggerated. I ate plenty, just not as much as he did. I'm not six foot something and two hundred pounds. Don't you worry, I'm strong. I'll do fine."

"You'll do wonderfully." Marion nodded her approval. "I can't believe you found enough lettuce in the garden for a salad. What did you think about the rest of things out there? Can we leave the beets for a few days?"

Jaxi's face flushed at the mention of the garden. Involuntarily, her gaze swung to Blake's face. She had to stop herself from licking her lips as she admired the way his plain blue T-shirt stretched over his shoulders, tight over the firm muscles.

Soft laughter rose from Matt.

"Yeah, Jaxi," Daniel said. "I wondered too. When you were in the garden earlier, did you see anything interesting? Anything that needed taking care of?"

Oh lordy, Matt and Daniel must have seen her gawking at Blake as he showered. An awkward silence hung in the air before she plucked up her courage. She grinned at Daniel. Might as well let them know right off the bat what her plans were. As far as she knew, those two boys wouldn't give her trouble. Heck, they might even support her.

"There're a few things looking mighty fine in the garden."

Matt choked on his drink and his shining eyes met hers. He raised his glass for a moment, then leaned forward to speak around Blake to Daniel. "Wonder what Jaxi's favourite vegetable is?"

"Carrots?"

"For better vision? I don't know, she's probably got pretty good eyesight already. Maybe the red-hot cayenne peppers?" Matt wiggled his brows, and Jaxi bit her lip and fought to keep from laughing.

"You think? Here I thought it might be the zucchini." Daniel started stacking empty plates together. "Course, the garden has such amazing views she—"

Jaxi rose quickly and went to the sideboard to serve the apple crisp. She'd been watching Blake out of the corner of her eye and knew the exact second he realized what the boys were teasing about. He didn't seem upset, more...distracted. She closed her eyes for a moment and drew in a slow breath.

He'd probably never thought about her that way before. He needed some time to realize little Jaxi was all grown up, and it was fine for her to admire him as a woman admires a man.

Hmmm. Maybe he needed a chance to do some admiring of his own.

Blake and Joel finished hauling the last of the order into the crate and wrapped it carefully. A few years back, neighbours had asked their dad to make them sets of the log furniture he'd filled the house with. One thing led to another, and the handcrafted items had become a huge success with people living in Canmore and Calgary. Now in their spare time, the Coleman boys took turns creating the solid log bed frames, tables and other household items. Most of their work was done in the winter when field chores were slower, but there was a constant trickle of orders they filled throughout the year to keep their name in the community.

Blake helped, although building furniture wasn't his favourite thing. He preferred outdoor chores or working with the animals. Daniel and the twins were more into the woodworking, but as a part of the family business he did his share to get everything done.

Besides, tonight it was mindless labour, and after sitting the whole meal across the table from Jaxi, he needed a little mindless.

Since their disastrous trip home a few years back, he'd tried his best to avoid her. She spent so much time with the Coleman clan, it hadn't always been possible. She was invited to birthday parties and holiday dinners, like she'd been since she was a little tyke. He worked hard to never be alone with her, always the first to leave the room and get chores started. Although he ached to touch her, all the reasons he had to stay away seemed more valid than ever. She was just a baby, barely twenty-one, while he was over thirty. She still looked up to him like a little sister to a big brother.

When she and Travis had broken up, Jaxi had gotten real busy with school and work, even though she hadn't left the community. She'd never mentioned anything about the ride with him, and Travis hadn't said a word about any strange farewell message from Jaxi, so Blake assumed she either didn't remember or just thought it was a fever-induced dream.

A dream. That's where the memories haunted him the most. He still woke in the middle of the night, picturing those wide grey eyes looking into his as her body pressed intimately close. Woke up armed and dangerous and no amount of cold showers stopped the wanting.

Now she was in his house, in the room next to his. What was his ma thinking to let a girl sleep in the basement with three grown men? Not only was he next door to her, but Matt and Daniel slept downstairs temporarily as well. If they were still living at the Peter's on the east section of the ranch, this whole situation wouldn't be nearly as complicated. Blake now wished like hell they'd never agreed to rent the house to that single mom for six months.

Sleeping would be tough, but supper tonight—watching her lick the stew off her fork—was another kind of torment altogether. He'd only had brief touches of what her mouth and tongue could do, and he wanted another round and more. More of Jaxi touching him, loving him.

More of what he could never have.

"What's the long sigh for, Blake? You feeling sentimental about shipping our trees to somebody else's house?" Joel asked as they finished packing the furniture into a crate, hammering the lid in place.

Blake looked up in surprise. "Did I sigh?"

"Like a dog that's been run ragged all day and just flopped down in front of the fire."

"It's nothing."

"It's Jaxi, I bet." Blake jerked. Joel leaned back on the worktable, his arms crossed in front of him and a knowing expression on his face. "Listen, Jesse told me to talk to you, so remember if you have the urge to punch me out you have to save half of the pounding for him. What do you think of Jaxi?"

Blake hesitated. What could he say in response to that kind of open-ended question?

"She's a good friend and it's going to help Ma a great deal to have her here. I appreciate her kindness." He looked around the shop for something to do with his hands. There was no way he could stand here and talk about Jaxi without fidgeting, and Joel was no dummy. He'd know Blake was pissing into the wind with his "good friend" comment if he fidgeted.

"You sure?"

"Why are you asking?" Blake found a table leg that needed hand sanding, and he sat to smooth the piece as he spoke.

"He's asking because he and Jesse are hoping to sweet-talk the girl into kissing them. I'm right, ain't I?" Daniel asked, joining them in the workshop.

Joel grinned. "We want more than kisses, but I'd settle for starting there. She's the sweetest kisser—"

"How do you know?" Blake demanded.

Daniel snorted. "You missed that one? The boys hogtied her back in high school, what was it, tenth grade? I heard about it for weeks, couldn't get them to shut up about how much fun they'd had, how soft her lips were, how she fit between them so well." Daniel shook a finger at Joel. "This habit you two have of going for the same girl at the same time isn't very socially accepted around these parts, you know. You better step real careful around the girls' daddies until you know for sure they don't plan to shoot one of you."

"You say that as if we're the only ones in this family who've shared a woman. Bullshit on that."

Daniel grinned. "Yeah, well, that might be true. But you boys take it to the extreme—do you even know what to do with a woman without a backup?"

Joel shot him the finger, and they both laughed.

"You and Jesse kissed Jaxi? At the same time?" Blake was still reeling from the thought. "Was this before or after she went out with Travis?"

"Before." Joel plopped on the bench next to Blake. "I still don't understand why she ever dated him. I know he's our brother and all, but sometimes he's such an ass. Of all the guys she could have gone to Grad with, why'd she pick him?"

"I still don't believe she kissed you and Jesse. Together."

"Well, it wasn't her idea, Blake. We were rather insistent. And she kissed us one at a time. It's not as if I want my lips right next to Jesse's. I'm not into that."

Daniel sat across from them on a stool and joined in. "I kissed her once." Blake barely stopped his jaw from hitting the floor. "Yup, only it was kiss her or kill her. She rode Thunder without permission, and when she managed to get him back into the barn without getting killed, I kind of lost my head." Daniel winked at Joel. "You're right, she is a sweet kisser."

Joel poked at Blake. "You ever kiss her?"

"No! Course not. She's just a little girl. I'm surprised at you, Daniel. She's five years younger than you."

"If I had been fifteen and her only ten, it would be have been a problem," Daniel said. "She was old enough and she knew what we were doing. I didn't give her much choice in the matter either. Looks like you're the only Coleman boy she hasn't kissed yet, Blake. Maybe we'd better set you up or something."

Joel bristled. "Hey, Jesse and I—"

"When did Matt kiss her? He's been going with Helen forever," Blake interrupted. All his brothers had kissed her. He didn't quite know what to think. He didn't expect her to be some kind of saint who'd never kissed anyone, but...all five of them?

"Oh, that. Matt kissed her when she was thirteen. She told me about it." Joel shrugged. "We were all down at the swimming hole, and Travis was teasing her how she didn't need to wear a girl's swimsuit yet, that she could still join them like she had as a little tyke, shorts and nothing else. Matt stopped the ass from being himself, then escorted her home. Jaxi told me he talked about changes, and how she would be a beautiful woman and not to worry when and where things would grow. Then he kissed her. She didn't remember exactly what he said because she'd been surprised but it was something about a kiss for the woman she was going to become."

"You talk to her a lot, Joel?" Daniel asked.

"Until she finished school. She's been so busy since, it's been like trying to track wildfire. Now that she's here, right in the house with us, Jesse and me figured it was a good time to make a move. We're all old enough."

"Old enough for what? You weren't planning to do anything under Ma and Dad's roof you wouldn't do in front of them, right?" Daniel demanded.

Blake kept his lips buttoned tight. The thoughts flying through his brain weren't suitable for speaking out loud. Jaxi had kissed them all. Except him. He picked up the smooth leg and deposited it with the rest of the wood. He needed a ride to clear his mind.

"Blake, you ain't told me yet what you think."

"About...?"

"Jaxi and Jesse and me."

Blake stopped and stared at his little brother. "Why are you asking me? She's the one that's got to decide if she wants you."

Joel glanced quickly at Daniel before he spoke. "We like her, and we want to see if she likes us. But if you ask, we'll wait until you get a chance first."

"What? What makes you think...?" This conversation had taken a turn for the worse, and fast. "Just because I'm the only one in the family who hasn't kissed her—"

"Blake, I know you care for her. A lot."

"She's too young for me. Be my guest and go for it, I don't think of her that way." *Sweet mercy, what a bunch of bull.* He thought of little but Jaxi. It was no use though. She was too young. She still looked up to him as a big brother, and he wasn't going to step over that boundary like some hormone-crazed animal. Blake ignored his aching gut and turned to head out the door when Joel called after him.

"You're lying through your teeth."

Blake paused and shook his head. "Am I now?"

"Damn right, you are. You remember camping in the back fields during calving season?"

"Yeah."

Joel jostled past him and paced backward for a few steps to stare Blake in the eye. "You talk in your sleep. You haven't kissed the girl, but don't lie about how sweet she is to you. Think on it and let me and Jesse know when you've made up your mind. Only don't wait too long or we'll decide for you. One way or another."

Chapter Three

"Oh God, oh God, *yeah.*"

Matt groaned out his agreement as Helen dragged her nails down his back, her body writhing under his. "Come on, baby. It's good, isn't it?"

She whimpered lightly, a sheen of sweat glowing on her skin from their fooling around, and Matt smiled. Yeah, she was close. After nine years together, off and on, there was no mistaking the signs. He knew by the tightening of her neck muscles, the soft moans escaping her lips, along with the increase in pressure where her nails dug into his shoulders.

He canted his hips to the left on the next thrust, opening up enough room to slip a hand between their bodies. When he touched her clit she jerked, then let loose a cry of approval as her sheath squeezed his cock tight.

"Matt, *ohh...*"

He dropped his head to her shoulder and buried himself deep, welcome relief and intense satisfaction hitting as his release jolted from his body.

It had been too damn long.

He was still brain-fuddled when Helen squirmed and pressed him away. "I need to pee."

Matt laughed. "You're so romantic."

She wiggled her brows. "I try."

The mattress dipped as he rolled and collapsed onto his back, muscles quivering. Helen scrambled upright and off the bed, and he watched her butt flex as she moved away from him toward the bathroom. Every curve of her body so familiar and attractive. He hadn't had enough of her yet.

"You want to grab some dinner at Casey's?" Helen asked, her voice carrying from around the corner.

No. Heading out was the last thing he wanted right now. "I already ate with the family. I can make you something here if you're hungry."

"I'd love a burger, and there're none in the freezer. I need to go shopping in the morning. Karen was supposed to stock up before she left." The toilet flushed and the water in the shower turned on.

Matt sat up, a rumble of discontent hitting as he dealt with the condom. After two months apart, he wanted a little more time alone with her before he had to start sharing again. He'd been thrilled to see the message she was back in town, rushing over as soon as he could get away from the family. "I don't mind hitting the store. Want me to run out quick and bring something back?"

There was no answer. She was probably under the water, the noise interfering with his question. Matt shoved off the bed and strolled to the door of the bathroom. Hmm, there were other ways to get her attention. He tugged the curtain aside, admiring how her muscles flexed as she washed, swirling the sponge over her tanned skin. There were all kinds of things he could do to her wet body. "Want some company?"

She shut off the water, already reaching past him for her towel. "Nahhh. I'm starving, and I promised the gang we'd meet them in a bit."

Frustration made his words harsher than he intended. "Shit, Helen. You're back in town for a couple hours and we're already heading out? I hoped we'd get some more time to catch up."

She stopped in the middle of rubbing her hair with the towel, her mouth arranged into a delicate pout. "You sex fiend. Haven't had enough yet?"

Fuck. He hadn't come over with the intention of falling into bed. At least not first thing—that had been her idea. "That's not what this is about."

Helen pressed her naked body against his, and his instant response put lie to his words. She stroked a hand over his cock and raised her brows, the smooth arcs perfectly in place. "It's okay. I'll be game for more later. I just want to see the gang. I've been gone all summer working, and I missed them."

His sigh escaped involuntarily. "I missed *you.*"

She relaxed against him, all familiar curves and well-known touch as she reached out to capture his waist. "I missed you too."

They stood for a moment, and the tension between them faded slightly. Matt breathed in deep, soaking in her scent, the rightness of having her back in his arms. The awkwardness was normal after being apart. And since neither of them was any damn good at emailing or phoning, not with the ranch chores or her remote summer job at the kids' camp, it had been a long time.

He had to show more patience, although that's all he ever seemed to do with Helen. Even making the moves on her the first time—he'd planned it for days before getting up the nerve. It had been worth it. Their first kiss had been magical, stolen by the bleachers at the high school between football practice and chores.

He smoothed her wet hair away from her face, "You remember our first time?"

Helen kissed his chest, running her fingers lightly over his ass. "Sweet sixteen and fumbling around in one of the trailers in the back of the ranch. You were so scared we were going to get caught."

That wasn't all of it. "I was scared I was going to blow before I got in you, let alone make sure you enjoyed yourself."

She scratched him as she pulled away, mischief in her eyes. "I always enjoy myself with you, Matthew Coleman. First time to now, you are one fine lover."

Happiness welled inside, covering some of his earlier frustration. "I love you, you know. Not just love having sex with you."

She blinded him with her smile. "You're kinda my favourite fellow as well."

A sharp tug hit his gut. She never said the words. Never said *I love you* back to him. "Someday you're going to forget and actually admit you're crazy in love with me."

Helen yanked on her clothes, her mischievous expression teasing him. "Now, Matt, they're only words. I don't deny you turn me inside out with lust, and spending time with you is one of my first choices. But I don't think love—"

"Is real, or forever? I know." He dragged a hand through his hair and headed for the shower. Since it seemed they were going out on the town, he'd better get cleaned up as well. He couldn't leave this conversation at that, though. She had to get past this issue at some point. "Just because your parents called it quits doesn't mean love isn't real. Look at my folks. Look at lots of couples right here in Rocky."

He rinsed off quickly while Helen used the mirror, talking over her shoulder. "Yeah, but my folks didn't call it quits, they

48

blew up world war three around us. Their split was more than nasty, it was mean. If that's how they could act after nearly twenty-five years together, and always saying 'I love you' to each other all the time? Total bullshit."

Matt grabbed a towel. Having this discussion again caused extreme frustration because nothing ever seemed to change. "I hear you. I still wish..."

He trailed off as Helen turned to face him, arms crossed in front of her chest. "Matt, I'm not ready to commit to anything else. Now I'm hungry, and you promised me burgers. We can talk about this in a few days when I've got myself back on a regular schedule. Two months of s'mores and campfires every night is more than one woman should have to bear."

"Does that mean a discussion about us moving in together will be happening sometime after burgers and seeing the gang?"

Helen stared, the naughtiness in her eyes as she looked him over making him regret having agreed to going out. "I have to admit knowing I would get to see more of this view regularly is a positive incentive to that idea. Now get cracking."

He snagged his clothes from the floor where he'd tossed them in his hurry to get naked. "Was that a yes?"

"It's a maybe. Dammit, Matt. I've been tossing and turning on a wooden-slatted bunk for months. Eating wieners and beans and way too many marshmallows. Food before serious conversations, all right?"

He backed down. Hell, he could see her point. When he came in from finding calves or working the far fields for weeks, all he wanted to do was sit and toss back a couple of cold ones and vegetate in front of the idiot box. There was something to be said for batching it with his brothers at times. They understood completely about having not even one more iota of energy left to be civil, let alone be caring and giving.

He grabbed his jacket and ushered her forward. "Deal. I'm officially moving that discussion onto the future list. I'll give you a little time."

When she would have danced out the door, he tugged her to a stop. Held her against him tight as he planted a huge kiss on her mouth, tender but firm enough she couldn't avoid him without really kicking up a fuss. He kissed her until the tension drained away, and she was all soft and warm in his arms.

Helen smiled sweetly, licking her lips, her gaze darting over his face. "Well. That was a lovely welcome home."

"That was the intention. I'm glad you're back, darling."

He held her close for another moment, their hearts synchronizing as they stood together in the gathering darkness.

Yeah. She was back and maybe this time he'd be able to find a way to convince her that what they had was good enough to take a chance on. To move beyond being good, to being even better.

Jaxi was grateful Marion didn't rise at five a.m. like usual to start her day. Maybe it was the painkillers, or sheer exhaustion, but the boys were already fed and watered and headed out for their day before Jaxi had to switch into her nursing role.

"We need to go to town today and hit the thrift shop, Mrs. C." Jaxi helped the older woman out of her husband's robe and into the tub. She set up a few towels to keep Marion's cast dry, then stepped back to give her privacy. "You can't wear oversized clothes until you heal, and I don't think we should cut up all your regular clothing so your arm will fit."

Marion sighed. "It's a little like trying to stick toothpaste back into the tube. You're right, we can go this afternoon. What else are you up for today?"

Jaxi paced around the room, making it as one-handed-friendly as possible. "I can do whatever you tell me needs doing. I'm here for you, to make things easier. Cook, clean. There are vegetables in the garden to harvest soon, and the apples you picked before you fell. You want those canned or dried? I didn't plan on making coffee and sitting around all day. I never have enjoyed lazing."

Marion went through a list of harvest items she had planned on doing that week. Jaxi listened even as she stopped to admire the family picture on the dresser, the six boys ranged in a circle surrounding their parents.

She had missed so much as an only child. Her folks loved her but didn't understand her need to be around others. They were both quiet, independent people who shied away from social events and thought nothing wrong with their little girl spending evenings and weekends alone with a book. When they moved to Rocky Mountain House and her new neighbours had welcomed Jaxi in, it was like she'd come home. All the time she'd spent at the Colemans' ranch over the years had opened her eyes and heart to the love of a big family.

The expressions on Mike's and Marion's faces in each picture displayed around the room made her heart skip. She saw it, plain as day. They were a team, loving and supporting each other as they worked the land and raised their family. Jaxi had seen that strength in Blake, and she wanted to show him she could create the same kind of team with him. The physical attraction she had for him was one thing, but his responsible character impressed her even more. The kind of a connection his parents had was what she longed for, ached for.

What she was willing to work for, body and soul.

She fell back into the routine of nursemaid easily, guiding Marion from the tub, helping her dress. Marion smiled approvingly. "Tell you what. Let's have a cup of tea, and we can plan the menus and a bit of a schedule for the next week so I can get those boys of mine to chip in as well."

"They don't need to help."

"Yes, they do." Marion waved her good finger in Jaxi's face. "I'm their mama, and if I tell them to help dry the dishes once in a while, it won't kill them. I don't expect them to do a lot, only a few things so you and I can get by. It's not as if they haven't been doing it on their own anyway."

"True, but—"

Jaxi rushed to help her as Marion got tangled in the sweater she attempted to lay across her shoulders. The older woman growled her frustration. "I still don't believe it. The house hasn't been this full in years, and now is when I had to go and hurt myself?"

"Oh, right. I'm sure you went and broke your arm just because. Accidents happen."

"Not to me." Jaxi bit her lip to stop from laughing as Marion's face changed from indignation to an embarrassed flush. "Listen to me, I sound like a baby, complaining because I'm a little inconvenienced. You're right. I didn't plan it, and we'll have to make the best of it. But that doesn't mean you're allowed to martyr yourself for me, young lady."

Jaxi backed down, or at least pretended to. She'd do what she thought was right when it came to getting work accomplished anyway—what Marion didn't see wouldn't hurt her. "No, ma'am. Boys can help out if you insist."

"And I won't have you scrubbing and such. Mike already said he'd get the Wilson woman to come in a couple of extra

52

times to do the floors. She usually comes once a week, so it's not much of a change for her."

"I really can do that. Honest."

Marion shook her head firmly. "You're a hard worker, Jaxi. But cooking and caring for a family this size takes a lot of time and energy. I'm going to need extra help since I can barely comb my hair by myself yet. I don't want to scare you away."

Little chance of that ever happening. "I think we'll figure things out."

"Come on," Marion said, grabbing Jaxi by the arm. "Let's go get that cup of tea."

Chapter Four

Blake pulled in next to the barn, his truck coated in dust. The west fields were bone dry, and he'd been driving all morning on bumpy back lanes. He stopped to take a swig of cold coffee from his thermos, distracted by a blonde head bobbing to the right of him as Jaxi walked the path to the chicken coop, her hands full of boards and tools.

Intrigued, he slipped from the truck and followed her, his eyes mesmerized by the sight of faded jeans cupping her trim ass as it swayed from side to side. She dropped her armload outside the wire surrounding the coop structure and snuck into the yard with an experienced air, shooing the chickens before her into the enclosure. Once she rounded them up, she closed the door firmly and spun to fetch her tools.

A flush crept over her skin as she spotted him standing beside the fence watching her. Then she grinned, and he reacted involuntarily to how her smile lit up his heart.

His whole body ached.

"What you doing?" He had to get a handle on himself. This is what he'd been trying to avoid, being alone with her. The setting was far from intimate and should be safe, but the edge of uncertainty was there.

Any situation with Jaxi was potential trouble as far as he was concerned.

She pointed to a section of the fencing that had worked loose, a hole dug partway under the wire. "Someone's trying to make a break for it, either in or out, and I don't want to wander the ranch looking for eggs." She propped open the gate and reached for the boards at his feet.

"You don't need to do that. One of us will fix it. Ma never told us there was a problem or we'd have done it already."

She leaned on the gate, her bright eyes sparkling at him. "I know you can fix the hole, but so can I. The sunshine is nice, and getting into the yard for some fresh air feels good." She waved the hammer at him briefly. "You go ahead and get your work done. I've got this under control."

Blake shifted back on his heels, a grin sneaking onto his face as he watched her haul the boards beside her and kneel to tackle the stiff chicken wire. She did know what she was doing—pulling the staples while holding the wire in place, twisting the hammer with enough leverage the wire popped into line rather than rolling away from her. The sun shone off her skin, a dusky tan showing on the muscles of her arms as she worked.

Jaxi glanced over her shoulder as she leaned back on the hammer, loosening an exceptionally tough staple. "You done with work for the day or what, Blake Coleman? Or have you never seen a fence fixed before so you want to learn some tips from me?"

She winked.

Minx. "Well, I haven't seen you fix a fence in a long time, Slick. Maybe you do it differently nowadays."

The hammer jerked and slipped from her grasp, her body falling back to land hard on her ass in the middle of the hen-scratched dirt. Blake stepped forward quickly to help her, and she chuckled, brushing the dirt from her jeans as she smiled sheepishly. "Maybe I do."

He checked to make sure she wasn't hurt. Seeing nothing but amusement in her eyes, he joined in the game. Nodding seriously, he teased, "I'm sure the last time I fixed a fence I didn't end up on my backside, but I suppose this method is more modern and sophisticated." He tugged the hammer she'd retrieved from her fingers and scooted around to remove the final staples, handing them one at a time for her to hang on to.

It was as if they'd gone back to the days when Jaxi would follow him around the farm all summer long, talking her head off about everything and anything. They worked together, putting the new boards into place and pounding in a stake to hold the chicken wire tight to the ground. All the while, Jaxi shared stories about taking care of the doctor's little ones, and her work at a local greenhouse the past spring. She even rambled about a book she'd just read that taught how to build a fishpond.

"That's interesting, but we don't need to stock a pond around here. It's a short ride to the river and part of the fun of fishing is heading out to somewhere unsoiled and untouched by human hands to sit for a while." Blake tugged on her ponytail gently like he used to when she was a kid. It had been good to work with her for a few minutes doing an everyday task. Something about it eased the tension within him, and for the first time in a long time, he simply enjoyed her company as he had for many years before his unspoken sexual longings had come between them.

Jaxi snorted. "You don't need to stock a pond, but the Mitchells are considering it. I promised to head out there next Saturday for a bit and see if I can help them get things ready. You want to come along?"

Blake nodded slowly. "I think I should be able to. Ask me later and we'll see what's on the schedule."

Her grin lit the whole area and Blake's heart gave a leap. All his calmness left abruptly. He squatted to gather the tools together, and their hands bumped as Jaxi grabbed for the hammer and clasped his wrist instead. Heads close, bodies near enough her scent filled his head and his body tightened with need. This was no little tagalong girl at his side, no matter how much he wanted her to be. No matter how much safer it would be.

Jaxi stared at him, and her pink tongue snuck over her bottom lip to moisten the smooth swell. Blake bit back the urge to lay his mouth on hers and lick over the wetness, tasting her skin and her sweet flavor. He needed to retreat, needed to stand and flee from temptation and the heavenly smell of her warm breath on his skin before he did something they would both regret. But heaven help him if he could budge.

She released her fingers slowly, drawing back with a butterfly softness that stroked up his arm and zipped back down in a direct line to his cock. Jaxi stood quickly, her hip bumping him hard, and Blake fell backward in the dirt. He stared into her laughing eyes.

"Why, Blake. You do know how to fix fences the modern way after all." Jaxi's skin remained flushed but her smile was innocent as she gathered the scrap lumber and loose staples. "Can you let the chickens out before you leave, and return the tools? I've got to get dinner on the table."

She waved briefly at him before she headed back to the house, whistling. Blake chuckled as he sat and watched her go. Wasn't her fault his body slipped into overdrive every time she got near. He needed to tamp down those feelings that should never have surfaced in the first place. Maybe this would work, like in the old days, and he would look out for her, as a big brother should.

He spotted the time and swore, scrambling to his feet to finish his work in a rush before dinner.

Chapter Five

Jaxi eased the heavily laden cart around the corner of the grocery aisle, finally headed for the checkout. A brief glance at her watch warned she had an hour—hour and a half at the most—before Marion got home for a rest.

An hour to get things put away so Marion *would* rest instead of attempting to help. She chuckled to herself. Mrs. C was a lousy patient, probably because she had rarely had a chance to slow down while chasing after the boys and taking charge of things. Jaxi stacked the cart contents on the conveyer belt as rapidly as possible and smiled at her friend Cari, who manned the till.

"Jaxi, you having a party or something? You've got enough food here to feed an army. Oh, hang on, you're at the Coleman place, aren't you?" Cari rang through the items, her mouth and hands in a contest to see which could move faster. "Course I figured you'd help, what with being neighbours and all."

Cari winked at her but Jaxi shook her head.

"Don't push it, girlfriend. Just get me through double quick so I'm back before Marion gets home and decides to scrub walls or rearrange furniture. It's been a week since she got the cast on, and she's attempting to take on her full workload again."

"Typical for her, though. Hey, are you going to be busy, or are we heading out tonight for our usual R and R?"

"I don't think I'll make it, if that's okay with you. I want to stick close so I can sit on my patient if she needs controlling."

Cari shrugged. "Fine with me, I'm free all weekend. We can meet whenever."

Jaxi paused in the middle of shuffling loaded bags back into the cart. "You're free? What about Leo and the big date? That's Saturday night, right?"

Her friend sniffed. "Wrong. He messed up one time too many. I'm done with him. *Jerk.*"

Jaxi hid her smile. Cari and Leo, the ultimate star-crossed lovers. A week didn't pass without one pissing the other off, and yet they couldn't stay apart. "What did he do this time?"

Cari propped her fists on her hips, her jaw hanging open. "You didn't hear? He went trolling with those wild Six Pack twins, and they weren't down by the lake from what I heard. They were fishing for females barely above the legal limit."

Something was off in Cari's information. That wasn't Leo's style, nor the twins. Women chased after Jesse and Joel. They didn't need to prowl to find willing partners. Besides, Leo was rock solid when it came to Cari, but the two of them didn't communicate and assumed far too much. "When was this?"

"Two nights ago. Marcy told Karen who told Janice she saw them."

Jaxi fought back the urge to rub her temples. "Cari, the boys were home two nights ago. All night. Jesse and Joel suckered us into a Monopoly tournament and a game of Thirty-one that lasted until late. Everyone crashed after it was done."

Cari's mouth closed tight. "You're not just saying that? I mean, to protect someone, 'cause I'd be really pissed to find out—"

Enough. Cari could rant for hours, and Jaxi's spare time was fading away. She handed over cash for the bill. "Trust me. Games all night and a popcorn fight when Mr. C lost his last penny. The man is a hoot—he cheats at cards like a shark, then distracts everyone. I don't know where Leo was but I doubt he was anywhere near any jailbait. He loves you, girl. Just call him and ask him. Go out on Saturday. Have fun."

Cari slipped from behind the counter to hug her, and Jaxi squeezed her briefly before whirling to escape the store. She'd arranged for Marion to have coffee with a couple of the ladies from the church. They'd return to the house far too soon. The clock ticking, Jaxi shoved the cart outside and looked around for the truck.

"You need a hand?" Jesse pushed off the wall, his bright gaze trailing over her with admiration as he sauntered closer. His sexy drawl was nice, but it simply didn't create the same chills big brother Blake's rougher tones conjured.

"Are you my ride? I want to beat your mom home."

Jesse shook his head sadly, his arms reaching around her to pull out a bag of M&M's. "Sorry, I'm meeting Joel to buy some supplies for the workshop. You're making Blake's favourite cookies this afternoon, aren't you? I like peanut butter better."

He lingered in her personal space, opening the bag and offering her a candy. Jaxi let a sigh loose from deep within her. He was incorrigible. "You want to move it or lose it? I'm not interested, Jesse, I told you before."

His gaze continued to caress her body. "That was a long time ago, almost a whole week. Maybe I can change your mind. There's no harm trying."

Jaxi prodded her thumb into his chest, snickering at his hopeful expression. He was damn sweet, but he wasn't Blake. "There's harm if I decide to lift my knee abruptly."

Jesse danced backward and shook his finger in her face, his grin stretching from ear to ear. "You don't play fair."

She raised a brow at him. "Nope, I don't. I play to win. Remember that."

A truck horn blared, and one of the Coleman trucks slid up to the curb, Blake's dark expression framed in the window.

"You needed a ride?"

Between the three of them the grocery cart was quickly emptied, and Jesse handed Jaxi into the passenger side before waving farewell. Blake peeled away, tires squealing, and Jaxi looked over her shoulder to see Joel join Jesse, the twins disappearing into the hardware shop.

She dropped her head back for a minute, closed her eyes and rubbed at the tight muscles in her shoulders. The past few days had rushed by in a blur. Marion's warning that the workload for a family of eight, nine with Jaxi added, was hellish had been a complete understatement.

Jaxi loved every minute of it.

They were halfway home, sitting in what she thought was a companionable silence, before she turned to Blake. "Thanks for the lift. I hope I didn't pull you away from something."

He shook his head. "Had to drop off a delivery at the post office." His lips clamped shut and Jaxi frowned. What bee did he have up his butt? Must have been a rush order or something.

"Jesse and Joel told me earlier you boys are playing pool tomorrow night." She stretched her shoulders and neck slowly, working out the kinks.

He kept his gaze on the road. "Yeah."

"Pass on a message to Leo for me? Cari's feeling neglected, and he'd better not cancel his Saturday night plans or she's going to give him hell. In fact, he might want to make sure it's an extra special evening to smooth things for a bit."

Blake grunted but otherwise didn't respond.

Jaxi frowned at him, his reaction baffling. "What? What's that look for?"

"Listen to you, handing out romance advice. Leo and Cari are old enough to take care of themselves. They don't need little girls telling them how to live."

Her jaw fell open, and she bit back the swear words she wanted to hurl. What the hell was he talking about? "I'm not a little girl, Blake. I'm twenty-one, and Cari and Leo are good friends of mine. I hate to see them screw up their relationship because they've forgotten to talk to each other."

"I still say it sounds ridiculous to hear you giving out advice on relationships and romancing. Leave them be." He took a corner too sharp and she collided hard with the side door.

"Slow down, Blake. What's gotten into you?" Jaxi had never seen him this way. He was pissed about something, and damn if she knew what it was. "I'm sorry if I messed with your schedule asking for a ride."

He glared at her for a second before his gaze darted away. "I said it was no trouble." He stared forward at the road. "You look beat."

She snorted. Good to know he found her attractive. "Thanks for the compliment."

"That's not what I meant," Blake protested. "You're burning the candle at both ends. Between helping Ma keep house and all the things you do in the community, you're working too hard. The phone's been ringing off the wall for you the last couple hours. A whole bunch of ladies called with information for the upcoming fall picnic, you got three calls from a guy named Royce, and the Taylors wanted to know if you could babysit for them tomorrow night."

Crap, no wonder he was upset. He'd spent the morning acting as her answering service. "Sorry, Blake. I told people to call my cell phone but the battery died. I guess since everyone knows I'm staying with you they decided to try the house. I'll tell them to stop."

"Who's Royce?"

She blinked in confusion for a moment. "Oh, a guy from college. He's trying to convince me to sign up for another class."

Why was he asking about Royce? Especially in that gravelly voice that made shivers scurry up her spine.

"The twins are already registered and ready to start. Can you still get into classes at this point?" Blake kept his gaze straight ahead on the road, but his hands hung on to the wheel a trifle tightly, his knuckles white.

Curiouser and curiouser.

The moment had come to be blunt. It was hardly right for her to fault Cari and Leo for not communicating when she was guilty of the same thing with Blake.

"I'm not interested in taking any more classes. I figure I need to move on to the next stage of my life. Meet new goals, fulfill new desires." Okay, it wasn't a totally blunt declaration of wanting to jump him, but it was a start. Especially as she opened her shoulders to face him, pulling one leg up on the bench seat so that her knee bumped into his thigh. A gentle caress. Barely there but enough to get her heart pounding.

"Where's he live?"

Her mind clouded with the image of Blake reaching to touch her, smoothing his strong fingers over her thigh. His work-hardened hands opening her jeans and unbuttoning her blouse, caressing her bare skin...

"Jaxi, where does he live?" Blake demanded.

She shook her head and lifted her gaze from his hands. *What the hell were they talking about again?* "Who?"

"This Royce guy."

The urge to giggle rose, and she beat it down unmercifully. Acting like a teenager wasn't the impression she wanted to project right now. "Don't worry about Royce. He's a nice enough guy but I'm not interested in him."

She adjusted her leg casually, rubbing his thigh again.

Blake changed gears, his leg shifting away from hers. "Well, you let me know if he gives you any trouble, alright?"

She leaned toward him slightly, letting her body soften, letting her desire for him show in her eyes and the tone of her voice. "Now why would you do that? You're not my father to watch over me and save me from the big bad wolves." *Come on, Blake, make a move.* She was sure she'd seen signs of his attraction, but the man was damn stubborn. Whatever held him back was driving her up the wall.

"No, I'm not your father, but I've thought about you a lot lately. I haven't been taking care of you as well as I did before you began college classes. I'm going to work on that, Jaxi. You need someone to watch out for you."

Hope rose in her heart. Was he coming around? Maybe his earlier anger was because he felt responsible for her and wanted more?

Then he dumped cold water on her dreams as he reached to pat her knee gently. Playfully. As far from a lover's caress as possible. "You're a good girl, and you deserve to be cared for. I'm going to be the best big brother you could ever have." With a final squeeze to her knee, he turned up the radio, and his strong hands thumped the wheel in time with the song, a peculiar pinched smile on his face.

Jaxi stared at him slack-jawed, her body and mind both reeling as she tried to understand what he'd just said.

He'd gone insane.

A big brother? Like *hell* that's what she needed. If he wanted to care for her, it wouldn't be as a big boy reluctantly playing house with a little girl. Making mud pies good-naturedly when he would prefer to be anywhere else. They'd done that already, years ago. It was time to shake things up, to show Blake she was no little girl and he was definitely not her big brother.

She'd told Jesse earlier she played to win. The game started now in earnest, and Blake wasn't going to know what hit him.

Chapter Six

The testosterone in the room was driving her crazy.

Jaxi dipped her hands into the sink and tested the water, turning her face away to hide the smile that rose unbidden as Jesse and Joel scrambled to impress her. They carried in dirty plates, scraping and cleaning the few leftovers into the slop buckets for the animals. They were well trained—Marion Coleman had never let any of her boys slack off, in or out of the house. Jaxi turned to the stack of hand washing and began.

If it hadn't been for the other chores, and helping Marion, she bet she wouldn't even be here now. Between the guys' skills at batching it, and the fact the twins would occasionally be home on weekends from school, there were a lot of hands around.

Just not enough when you added Marion's work to the list.

"You sure can cook up a storm." Joel nudged her hip lightly to get her to step aside as he rinsed one of the large roasters in the second sink.

"How come you seem to know how much to prepare to have enough for us all? You've only got three in your family." Jesse stacked plates in the dishwasher, standing to flash her a grin. "And for the record, I agree with Joel. That was great. Thanks."

She shrugged, rinsing bubbles from utensils and passing them to Joel to dry. "You're welcome. And I estimate, then double. You know, to be able to feed you two bottomless pits."

Their good-natured responses made her smile. That's what she wanted from them—friendly, not sensual. If she could just keep them on the right track.

"Hey, you guys looking forward to college? What you got on your schedule this semester?" Jaxi wasn't going to miss it. Not with the plans she was finally moving on, but there was a part of her that was real happy she'd gotten a chance to go for a few semesters.

"It's all awesome. The technology classes—so incredible what they've got set up for using with the crop rotations and helping with the planning." Joel leaned against the counter, the dishtowel fluttering in one hand as his face lit with excitement. "I've already managed to incorporate some of the information from last year into this coming season. I show Dad what I can as I learn it. By Christmas I hope to have more solid plans to be able to help arrange for our spring purchases."

Jaxi shook her head in wonder. "Computers and crops. Never thought that would happen."

"It's only a part of it," Jesse interrupted. "You wouldn't believe the genetics classes. That's my area of expertise."

The boys rambled on for a bit, enthusiasm and energy quivering through them. Jaxi wiped down the counter and began breakfast preparations. Marion had different methods, but since she'd taken over in the kitchen, Jaxi did things her own way. And her way involved planning ahead.

"One of you grab me the oats, please? Your mom said there's supposed to be a big bag tucked somewhere, but I can't seem to find it."

"I got it." Travis slipped in through the swinging door and tilted his head toward the pantry. "Last time we did groceries, I had to put it up on the top pantry shelf."

"Good timing, asshole. Dishes are nearly done." Jesse snapped his towel at his older brother as Travis paced past.

Travis spun out of the way and nabbed Jaxi, tugging her against his body to use her as a shield. "I was working."

"Working on skipping work."

Travis's forearm pressed hot against her belly where he held her close, dragging her across the room. "Now, now. I'm here and eager to be of assistance. Why don't you kids go do your homework or something, and I'll take good care of Jaxi for the rest of the night."

Oh brother.

"I don't think I need much taking care of." Jaxi tugged on Travis's arm until he released her. He turned to pull down a full twenty-five-pound bag of oats only after winking at her mischievously. This was a complication she hadn't expected. It was bad enough having to fight off the twins' attention, but Travis?

The boy didn't take no for an answer very easily. Come to think of it, none of the Six Pack boys did. Except Blake, damn it all.

Travis carried the bag to the counter while Jaxi grabbed the other supplies she needed, dragging a Crock-Pot over and loading it with the fixings for overnight cooking.

She was in the middle of measuring vanilla when he stepped behind her again, reaching around to grab the brown sugar. He adjusted the lid carefully, organizing her supplies. All the while far too close, rubbing and bumping her at every chance.

Double oh brother.

She glanced across the room. Yeah, the twins had noticed. Joel opened his mouth, probably to lambaste Travis. She moved to cut him off—Travis's damn competitive spirit would just encourage more attempts if Joel rubbed him wrong. It had taken a long time to figure out Travis's weak spots, but now that she knew what they were, she had no objection to exploiting them.

"If you're all going to hang out and get in my way, you may as well be useful. Jesse, grab me the eggs from the fridge. Joel, I need some cheese grated, about a cup, please. Travis, move your ass back two feet or I'll be using your balls for playing marbles."

Jesse snorted.

Travis scooted away. "You don't want to be doing that."

"Course she doesn't," Joel teased. "That would be like playing with peewees. Makes it tough to win anything."

Travis swung at his brother. Jesse moved forward and the wrestling began.

Jaxi ignored them—fighting between the boys was as regular as breathing. Didn't matter that they were now over six feet tall, just meant the crashes had gotten louder. She finished up a couple more things, weaving her way around the guys as they slipped into familiar routines of taunting and goofing off.

It was fun and relaxed, and all a part of the whole picture. Family. What she wanted so badly.

Joel handed her a dishtowel to dry her hands. He hung on to it for an extra second, catching her attention. He spoke quietly even as the other two kept up their lighthearted bickering in the background. "You okay?"

She smiled. "I'm great. Thanks for the help tonight."

Joel tilted his head toward the others. "You know, Jesse doesn't mean to be an idiot. Travis? I'm not so sure about."

Jaxi laughed. "I can handle them both. Thanks." Impulsively she leaned forward and kissed his cheek. "Breakfast at seven, right? That give you guys enough time to get where you're going in the morning?"

"More than enough." He grinned. "I'm glad you're here, Jaxi. And you need something, you be sure to ask, okay?"

She smiled, happy to have his support, even though the next part of her plan didn't require much but her and Blake and a little good timing. "I'll definitely keep that in mind."

Blake entered the house long after dark. He'd ridden until the cobwebs cleared from his brain. He'd cared for his horse and polished a couple of saddles in the tack room. Anything to keep his hands busy, anything to keep his mind off Jaxi and what her presence did to him.

It hadn't gotten any easier over the past week. Sitting across the table from her at meals, playing games as a family. Every time they bumped arms in a hallway, his damn cock stood up and took notice.

What a disaster. This whole mental shit storm—no matter how many times he went through alternatives, there was never a better solution to his dilemma. He couldn't act on his desire for Jaxi because it wasn't right. Thinking about her made need build deep in his core. She'd bolt like a wild horse if he even hinted at how much he wanted to seize total control over her body, touching her, taking direction over her pleasure.

The whole business of her dating someone else raised its ugly head again today with the calls from Royce. The third time the asshole phoned Blake actually growled before controlling

71

himself. Imagining her with anyone but himself made his stomach clench.

Yet if he didn't approach her, the twins would think they had the go-ahead to try and convince her to accept them. Seeing Jaxi with them today outside the store, even briefly, had made him pause. It wasn't that they weren't good enough. They were both smart, good-looking fellows who would care for her.

But—both of them?

Blake threw his coat on a hook and brushed his boots clean. Whatever made Joel and Jesse think double-teaming a woman on a constant basis was a good idea in the first place? How could they watch another man, even their brother, touch skin that had flushed under their fingers moments ago? Or hear the woman they cared for cry out as another brought her pleasure?

Could he stand it if Jaxi did hook up with one of the twins? To watch them cuddle and kiss in front of the family? It had been bad enough when she went out with Travis, and he'd rarely seen many signs of affection—let alone passion—between them. Blake's need to be with Jaxi seemed to grow instead of fade as time passed, and knowing his brothers were making love to the girl would just about kill him.

He ran upstairs and poured himself a glass of iced tea. The table was already set for breakfast, and in the kitchen three Crock-Pots lined the counter, filled with food to slow cook all night long. His ma used the pots once in a blue moon so this had to be Jaxi's doing. A slip of paper rustled on the bulletin board. A menu and a to-do list in her flowery print.

She didn't turn her dots into little hearts anymore.

Strolling through the quiet house en route to the basement, he spotted the twins, deep in conversation on the deck. They waved and he joined them, sitting with his back to the house to look out at the lawn and road, into the starlit sky.

"House is quiet."

"Jaxi made Ma take a couple of painkillers, and Dad said he'd hit the sack early to care for anything she needed." Jesse darted a glance at Joel. "Daniel said he was wiped from sitting in the sauna of a tractor all day, and Matt went out to spend the evening with Helen. They both disappeared some time ago."

"Where's Travis?" Blake asked.

Joel spat out a sunflower seed shell and grinned. "Him? He's pouting in his room."

"Pouting? What happened now? Dad ask him to deliver the shipment to Red Deer or something?"

Jesse sat back, side by side with Joel. It was like looking at mirror images. "Yeah, well, Dad did tell him he's on the broken tractor until further notice since it was his responsibility to arrange for the air conditioning to get fixed. But nah, this time he's pouting because of Jaxi."

"Because she's here?"

"Because she's here and treating him like he deserves." Jesse reached his arms in the air before easing them back and resting his head in his folded hands. "We all helped do the dishes after supper, and he was acting all sweet and dopey. She basically told him to stuff it."

Blake stiffened in his seat. "What'd he try?"

"Relax, Blake, it was fine. He was pretending to brush against her by accident, nothing too bad. The funny part was she didn't get mad, just told him off real matter of fact. Like we all knew he was an idiot so why should she waste energy getting upset."

Joel stood and stretched lazily. "Feels strange, all of us home and headed to bed early. You'd think it was ten years ago or something. Hey, the gang's meeting at Traders tomorrow. You're planning on going, right?"

Blake nodded slowly. "I told Leo I'd partner with him playing pool for the night. No use letting you boys retain the title any longer than we have to."

"You think your game is on enough to beat us?"

"Damn right it is."

Jesse swept the remainder of the sunflower shells into the dustbin as he gave Blake a cocky grin. "Hope you sleep well tonight. Get enough rest. You know, being you're so old and all..."

He danced out of Blake's reach. Joel snickered and hit his brother on the arm. "Lay off him. Night, Blake. Jaxi said breakfast at seven."

The twins slipped into the darkness toward the main floor room they still shared. Blake watched them go, caught by how much it was like hitting a time warp, seeing the house filled at every corner. Those two had been a handful as kids, but they'd turned into fine young adults.

If they didn't want Jaxi, he would have thought even better of them.

Blah. That was sour grapes on his part. If he couldn't have her—and he couldn't—maybe the twins were the best thing for her. *One* of them. Maybe.

Blake rose and made his way downstairs. His feet seemed to stop of their own accord five paces too soon. He stared at the door of the den, closed tight. Behind those doors Jaxi would be curled up, her blonde hair draped over the pillow, body nestled in the thick comforter covering the sofa bed. She probably wore one of those baby-doll nighties, her long legs exposed, her

74

smooth shoulders bare under thin straps of some kind of soft, shiny material. Sleeping in the room next to her the first night had been difficult, and after only a week, his desire for her had grown even stronger.

Blake bit back a growl and headed to his room. His ma needed the help but this week had been sheer hell on his body. Even now he was harder than a railway spike, the thought of Jaxi close by teasing his senses. He swore the scent of her filtered through the walls.

He stripped off his jeans and shirt, then padded toward the bathroom door. Fingers on the latch, he stilled. Oh hell, he'd nearly forgotten he couldn't go in. As the oldest son he'd taken advantage of picking the only downstairs bedroom with an attached bathroom. But it had a connecting door to the den as well, and Jaxi had all her things in there. He stood, his hand glued to the doorknob. He wanted to enter, even hoped by some chance she'd have left the other door open, and he could torment himself with a glimpse of paradise.

Blake dragged a breath of air into his lungs in an attempt to cool his burning body. This wasn't right. She was a guest in their home, and yet here he was, acting like a hound dog. He should be ashamed of himself.

He grabbed his travel kit and marched down the hall toward the large shower room in the annex. He, Matt and Daniel had promised to use the larger bathroom and let Jaxi have the privacy of the other for herself.

The sound of running water met his ears and Blake stepped into the dimly lit room, wondering why his brothers had turned on only half the lights. Splashing noises echoed. Leaving his kit on the sink counter, he rounded the corner to the showers.

And froze.

The three showerheads in the open room were separated by nothing but space. Steam filtered the dim lighting into a moonshine glow.

All he saw was wet, naked skin. Jaxi's skin. Every inch of her bare to his gaze as water poured from the middle shower, streaming in waves over her body. She faced away from him, head thrown back as she shifted to allow the water to slip over her face and down her chest. Blake, his body hot and needy, watched in a daze as the shampoo rinsed from her hair and undulated down her back, tiny bubbles racing over the curve of her waist. His gaze followed the bubbles along the gentle swell of her hips and the full curves of her ass. Her skin was pale pink from the heat of the water, faint tan lines showing on her thighs and arms.

His mouth went completely dry. Retreat. It had to happen— he had to turn and leave before she spotted him. Yet, no matter how loud his brain screamed at him, his feet remained glued in place as she slid the soap over her body. As she lifted her hands to brush her hair back from where it clung to her shoulders in white ribbons.

Blake's cock tented his boxers as Jaxi rotated under the showerhead, turning the front of her body to his sight. Her nipples were soft. Tender, juicy pink berries crowning full, taut curves. The perfect size to fill his hands and still allow him to take her into his mouth. Water slid in rivulets over her belly and through the pale blonde curls visible at the junction of the long legs he'd fantasized about so many times. Jaxi's eyes were closed, and she swayed as she washed, her hands slipping over her body in a way that made Blake heat to near boiling just from watching her. She hummed, quiet and low, her hips moving to the faint tune.

Guilt shot through him. He had no right to watch her, no right to invade her privacy and treat her like anything but the beautiful, caring person he knew her to be. She wasn't his to admire.

God help him, he wanted her to be.

He swallowed hard and tried to peel his gaze away. Tried to not watch as her hands covered her breasts, then slicked over her belly in slow circles. Tried to glance away as she slipped her fingers gently through the curls covering her pussy, over her ass, washing every inch of her luscious body clean.

Blake watched, motionless and noiseless for so long he felt like a statue, every bit of his body gone as hard and rigid as his aching shaft. Indecision held him, immobilized him. The rush of blood through his veins drowned out the part of his common sense saying he needed to leave. The pounding faded everything logical and rational away in him and stripped him bare to need and desire.

His eyes needed him to stay here, to fill his brain with the vision of her glowing skin, her seductive movements. His hands needed to touch her, run over her curves in imitation of the water caressing in endless sweeps. His mouth needed to taste— not only her lips, but her breasts and the spot on her back where the skin dimpled above her ass.

He desired her. Every fiber of his being wanted to show her how much, but his conscience kept kicking his feet from under him before he could cross the room.

This was *Jaxi*.

He wished he had never walked down the hallway.

Jaxi opened her eyes, her gaze unfocused for a second before she noticed him standing in the steamy room like some ghostly Peeping Tom. Her quick intake of breath showed clearly enough she didn't expect anyone, hadn't realized she'd been putting on a show.

Now was a perfect time for him to drop his head and slip away. He couldn't do it. She stared back at him through the mist hanging in the air, her eyes as big as silver dollars. She bit her bottom lip, and he fought a mental battle to leave, fought to stay quiet.

Then he noticed her nipples change. Tightening even as he looked at her. Electric pulses shot through him, and his hands itched to touch her, to lift the weight of her breasts and lap at those gems that had grown erect beneath his gaze.

Jaxi turned off the water and stepped slowly toward him, head held high. She sauntered up, slippery and wet, naked as a jaybird. Her skin glowed with heat as she stopped inches away, staring unendingly with those mesmerizing grey eyes. She reached out, her naked skin brushing his shoulder. She drew back, her arm clasping a towel she'd grasped from the hook beside his head.

He thought she'd wrap herself up quick. Instead she rotated her fingers and let the towel hang as she held the fluffy fabric to him. He glanced down, saw the way her hand trembled even as she put on a bold face and kept her body motionless under his heated gaze. He reached for her, his hand moving of its own accord before his brain fully engaged.

What brain? All the blood he needed for thinking had pooled in his groin.

This was the second time she'd taken him by surprise, and he couldn't make the same mistake. He'd been haunted since the first incident.

He couldn't let anything happen. It wasn't right for them to be together.

Blake withdrew his hand.

And fled.

Chapter Seven

The morning passed in a blur of activity. Jaxi cooked and cleaned with a vengeance, but deep inside a huge lump sat and burned at her innards. Blake hadn't said good morning to her. He'd avoided her gaze at breakfast and hightailed it from the house as quick as a jackrabbit. She wasn't sure what to do next because after she'd crawled into her bed last night she realized she'd been way out of line.

Apologize? That would be smooth. She could hear herself now. "Sorry for getting naked and hoping you'd ravish me in your parents' house with your brothers just down the hall."

Damn. How was she supposed to get him to make a move when they lived in the same house? With the whole family always around or popping up unexpectedly? As much as she loved his family, it was Blake she wanted.

This wasn't going to be as easy as she'd first imagined.

After dinner Matt tugged her aside. "You want to go to the children's summer theater performance at the community hall this Wednesday?"

She hesitated, panic flooding her. Not Matt too. Sweet, considerate, usually insightful Matt. He excited her about as much as a bouquet of dandelions. The expression on her face must have shown her fear because he chuckled and quickly reassured her. "I don't mean *with* me, Jaxi. Hell if you need that kind of complication in your life right now. Not to mention you know Helen would have my balls if I stepped out on her."

Her muscles unclenched slowly as he patted her shoulder. A pat from him felt proper, caring and supportive. It wasn't a cop-out like the treatment from Blake the other day. If any of the Colemans was a big-brother figure to her, it would be Matt.

"I'm already going to the hall on Wednesday," Jaxi said. "I promised to seat people and sell tickets for the raffle. Plus do cleanup after."

"Maybe you should have someone help you. I hear Blake is free on Wednesday, and I bet he would give you a hand if you asked."

Jaxi snorted. "You here on his behalf? I don't think your brothers are too shy to ask me if they want to do something with me, Matt. They're grown men, they've got tongues in their heads."

He stopped and stared out the window for a minute before he answered. "Well...yeah, we might be all grown, but that doesn't mean we can all see what's right in front of our noses. Some of us don't make the best decisions for ourselves because we try too hard to do what we think is proper for everyone else."

Cryptic, even for Matt. Jaxi leaned a hip on the counter. "Okay..."

He smiled before reaching to tweak her nose. "As for not being shy, you never know. Sometimes it's the biggest and seemingly boldest animals you've got to gentle along real slow and easy to get the right results. Too fast and they spook."

Her face flushed with heat, and she busied herself wiping the sink to avoid looking him in the eye. Oh lordy, did Matt know what had happened last night? How shockingly she'd behaved?

"If you have a little extra time this afternoon, you can switch your stuff into the far basement bedroom. Blake told me this morning he's taking the guest cabin so you can have a real bed, and we'll be able to use the office again."

Jaxi's heart choked off her throat. What had she done?

Matt watched her walk away, her expression of dismay showing all too clearly something had gone down sideways.

He stepped outside and sucked in a deep breath of the late August air. He didn't know if he should be happy that he wasn't the only one who had a setback last night or not. He didn't wish Jaxi and Blake anything but the best, even if it pissed him off royally that Blake had someone willing to show at every turn how much she admired him and the bastard kept pushing her away. Whereas he had someone he loved who simply wouldn't admit it back.

And then last night...

Fuck.

He drove to the north field to fix a pump that was acting up. Diving into a frustrated tussle with rusted pipes and broken water lines was preferable to the mental wrestling he'd been doing for the past twelve-plus hours.

A line of dust headed his direction, his cousin's shiny new Toyota drawing closer. Matt wiped the sweat from his brow with his shirtsleeve and waited for Gabe to park on the far side of the gate.

"Uncle Mike called. Said you've got a seized pump?"

"She's dead."

Gabe handed forward the replacement part Matt needed. "Just so happens I'm doing the same sorry task as you today. Want to work together? It'll save time."

Matt nodded. "I'd enjoy the company."

They worked easily together, slipping the new part into place and adjusting the attachments. Matt twisted the tap, and water filled the trough. "This one's done."

"You want to drop your truck at the main gate and use mine to work the fields?" Gabe asked. "I've got extra pumps with me, and tools."

Matt followed his cousin back across the field. The whole time his dilemma with Helen repeated like a scratched CD. He jumped into the cab with Gabe, momentarily distracted by the new vehicle. "Damn nice in here. You win the lottery or something?"

Gabe shook his head. "Just don't have to spend my money on keeping a woman happy, like you."

Fuckdamnshit. "Solo as always, hey, Gabe?"

"Damn right. I know what to do with a woman, but it's gonna take more than a sweet fuck to make me want to give up my freedom like you Six Pack boys seem bound and determined to do. I hear Blake's being pursued by Jaxi again. When he gonna give up running and lay down in defeat?"

"Hell if I know."

"Yeah, then there's Daniel. He still sweet on Sierra?"

Matt held tight to the roll bars as Gabe cleared the cattle gate en route to the next pump. "She ditched him a couple of months back. In the spring."

Gabe swore. "For serious? I hadn't heard that. Thought she was aiming to get him to the altar before the year was out."

Another woman Matt didn't understand. "Remember last winter when the mumps went through town? Daniel never had them as a kid and caught them."

"I remember."

"She got worried about him not being 'right' afterward and told him to get checked at the doctor."

Gabe snorted. "Not being right? What the hell was she worried about?"

Matt sighed. "Turns out Daniel's shooting blanks, and Sierra wanted a big family. She dumped him right after the results came in."

"That's fucked up. I thought that was usually the guy's deal breaker, not the girl's." Gabe shook his head, pausing the truck by another gate and waiting for Matt to hop out to open it. "Damn incredible the things some women get into their brain as to being important."

The words impacted harder than his cousin intended. Matt popped the wire at the top of the gate and dragged open the fence, closing it after the truck and pacing slowly forward to rejoin Gabe. It was a perfect opportunity to approach a very awkward subject.

He sat heavily, staring at his cousin for a minute. Gabe's side of the family was the blondest of all the Colemans. The girls in town were always raving about their angelic good looks. Yet, he knew without a doubt that Gabe had no interest in stealing his girl.

Matt dithered for another moment. There really was no way of saying this but straight out. "You ever done a threesome?"

Gabe hit the brakes a little too fast, jolting them both in their seats next to the pump. He frowned at Matt. "Where the fuck did that come from?"

"You mentioned the incredible things that women get into their heads. You won't believe the one Helen dropped on me last night."

"Threesomes? You guys got to talking about that?" Gabe undid his seat belt and whistled softly. "Hell, I figured with your family history you'd already been fooling around left, right and center with that woman."

Matt banged his fist on the dash before cracking open the door and grabbing their supplies. "Don't look at me for the freaky sex habits. Far as I know, it's only Travis and the twins who get off on having more than one person in their bed."

Gabe frowned. "Then if you're not interested in trying it, why—?"

"Because she asked me. Told me she was curious. We ain't..." Matt's throat choked up tight. Damn, it was nearly impossible to have this talk. What was it going to be like if he actually got up the nerve to let someone into the bedroom with them? "We ain't never been with anyone else, neither of us."

His cousin snorted. "Okay, sorry. Not funny when you're the one being jerked around, but from where I sit, this conversation is a ripper. You're telling me you've only had sex with Helen? Ever?"

Matt nodded.

"Shit."

They worked in silence for a couple of minutes, moving automatically to clear and repair the waterline. Matt rinsed off his hands and dried them on his shirt before standing and forcing the words out. "So, would you be interested?"

"For a piece of Helen?" Gabe nodded slowly. "Well, there's the instant reaction of 'hell yeah', but I'll be honest. The only way I'm willing to do this is if you're sure you're not going to want to kick my ass around for the next twenty years. You sure you want someone in her bed that you'll see forever?"

Matt had thought this through a million different directions. "Having a stranger touch her would be worse. From the grapevine gossip I figure you know how to treat a woman."

Gabe leaned back on his heels, his hat cocked to the side. His ever-present teasing grin had disappeared. "It must have rocked you hard to have her ask you for this."

"You have no idea."

"I don't, so let's say we make this conditional. You two think on it some more. If after you've had a chance to reconsider, she's still keen, then let me know." Gabe shuffled upright. "And Matt?"

"Yeah?"

"If this goes down? I promise I'll treat her good. And I'll never mention this conversation or what follows again, no matter what. Swear."

Relief streaked through Matt. "Appreciate it. All of it."

For the first time since Helen had made her request, he thought there might be something to look forward to. Making her fantasy come to life? Hell, he'd always thought he'd do anything for her.

Seems he was going to get the chance to prove it.

Chapter Eight

When Blake asked Jaxi if he could help her at the play, she wondered if Matt had manoeuvred the request. Still, by the time Wednesday rolled around and the performance was over, most of the awkwardness she'd caused by her boldness in the shower had faded. She wasn't any closer to getting Blake to acknowledge he wanted her, but at least they were talking again.

They cleaned together, brooms in hand, sweeping the nearly empty hall. She was right in the middle of planning her next step, wondering what words to use to follow Matt's suggestion of "gentling the shy animal along" when Blake dropped a bombshell.

"I've been thinking about the other day."

Lordy, so had she.

"This Royce fellow. How old did you say he is?"

She literally tripped over her own feet and landed on her butt. Did he just ask about Royce again? He wasn't talking about the shower at all?

The man had gone mad.

"I don't think I told you how old he is. What the hell does Royce have to do with anything?" She scrambled to her feet and brushed off her jeans. She'd spent the evening admiring how

Blake capably dealt with last-minute disasters for the theater company. Admired the way he visited with the townsfolk during the intermission, chatting and laughing with people of all ages. Admired the way he looked in his well-worn jeans, all muscle and tightly bound energy.

And now he wanted to talk about someone she knew from college? *Was he crazy?*

"I figured you two must have a lot in common, if you were in the same classes and all. Maybe it would be good for you to select another class or two and spend time with the guy. If he lives in the area you could call and ask him to join us for supper." Blake swept vigorously as he spoke, dust flying everywhere.

Jaxi dropped her broom and grabbed his with two hands, stilling his erratic motion. She jerked their bodies together so she could stare up into his face easier. He avoided her eyes for a moment before turning that ghastly smile on her, the one he'd worn ever since announcing he was going to be her *big brother*.

"Enough, Blake. You are seriously pissing me off and I want to know what your problem is."

He shrugged and attempted to remove the broom from between them. "I thought it might be nice, if you like the guy, for you to spend time together."

"I don't want Royce." Jaxi shook the handle violently before releasing the wooden shaft with a snap. She stepped back to glare at him, fists resting on her hips. "I want... Oh, damn it, do I have to spell it out for you? I thought it was pretty clear what I wanted the other night in the shower. I want *you*."

He shook his head and resumed sweeping, giving her no more attention than if she was one of the cats underfoot in the barn at milking time. "I'm too old for you. Heck, it's like I'm your big brother and—"

Jaxi ripped the broom from his hands and hurled it across the room. He was being a bloody jackass. It was a damn good thing she loved him because otherwise she'd be tempted to kill him.

"You are *not* my brother, by any stretch of the imagination. The things I want us to do, Blake, they are *not* brother/sister activities." She took a slow breath and calmed her temper. At least they were talking, even if Blake seemed to be speaking some weird foreign dialect and she didn't have a translation book.

Slow down. Go gently.

She had to get him to acknowledge what he wanted, not what he thought needed to happen. Get him to drop the damn sense of responsibility for long enough to see the real picture. Jaxi snuck in closer, resting a hand on his crossed arms. She drew a slow finger along his skin, speaking quietly. "You ever dream about me, Blake? You ever think about taking me in your arms and kissing me? Touching me? I dream about you all the time. You, in my bed, making me feel things I've never felt before."

"Stop it, that's not going to happen." Blake jerked away from her, and Jaxi's stomach lurched. He didn't even want her to touch him. "You're an attractive woman—"

Red flashed before her eyes. He was the most frustrating man she'd ever met. She followed him closely, crowding against his body. "Oh, now I'm a woman. Well, that's a plus. You finally noticed I grew up. What's the problem? I think you like me too, so why aren't we acting on the attraction between us? What's got you putting on the brakes when that's got to be the last thing you really want?"

Blake grabbed her by the shoulders and manoeuvred her away from him. He paced back, his hands dragging through his hair in frustration, swear words floating on the air. When he turned toward her, his face had gone grey and drawn, as if he'd shut off his heart. His gravelly voice cut deep as he spoke.

"The issue is you're still a little girl compared to me, and you won't be happy with an old man for long. Do I want you? Hell, yeah, you make my body ache so hard it's a fucking nightmare for me to wake and realize you're not really there. But I'm too old for you, and I refuse to take advantage of the physical pull between us for a one-night stand. Stop trying to seduce me and prove you're as grown up you claim. Find someone your own age to play with."

She gasped as pain rippled through her belly. His words lashed her, stinging to the core. The seemingly caring tone he delivered them in made it worse. She wanted to smack him hard enough to knock off his blinders and turn this disaster of a conversation around.

Before he broke her heart.

Anger made her retaliate in a whole new direction.

"Oh, so now I'm old enough to play around, just not with you. Hmm, let's see, who do I know that's around my age and interested in me. Gee, two names jump to mind."

"Jaxi..." The emotionless face before her changed instantly, disapproval and anger flashing one after the other.

"What, you don't think your little brothers are interested in me anymore? I'm pretty sure Jesse said he was, just the other day."

He stepped toward her, forcing her to shuffle backward to stay out from underfoot. "I've warned them you're off limits. The only way I want to see you around them is if you pick one and the other swears to bow out. I won't have you messing with them both."

Jaxi popped her eyes open wide and faked a delighted expression. "So the rumors are true, they do get involved with the same girl at the same time. Well, damn, that sounds like a bit of an adventure. Maybe that's what I need to distract me since I can't have what I want."

"You stay away from my brothers," he warned, his voice harsh and low.

She let out a burst of laugher, feeling hard and tight inside. "You're not the boss of me. Maybe I can't convince the one Coleman I *want* to be with me, but I bet you I sure as hell can have a little fun with a couple others."

He loomed over her, dark and dangerous, and she wanted to have him hold her instead of dealing with this whole stupid mess. "Let's not throw it away, Jaxi, all those years of friendship."

Her throat tightened up, anger melting away as she fought back tears. There was no way she would cry in front of him, not now. She had to figure out a solution to stop this train wreck from continuing. "I agree we've had something special in the past. But don't you see, all those years of friendship were leading to something bigger and better, and that's what you're choosing to give up on. You, Blake, you're the one throwing the possibility of us away. I know what I want."

She stood on her tiptoes and brushed a kiss on his burning hot cheek before whispering, "Let me know when you're ready to admit what you *really* want. I'm getting tired of waiting for the right answer."

Jaxi had never been keen on dramatic exits but time was of the essence to avoid bursting into tears in front of him. She slipped past his solid bulk and dashed out the fire exit.

Chapter Nine

Blake took another draw on his beer and placed the bottle down carefully before turning his attention back to the surface of the pool table. He and Leo were maintaining their own over the twins, the score sixty-seven to sixty-four. Better than the previous Friday when he'd still been out of his mind trying to understand what had happened with Jaxi in the shower the night before. Damn, his life had turned into a cheap dime-store romance gone sour.

Joel and Jesse relaxed nearby, cocky grins on their faces.

"Not bad for a tired old man," Jesse said, twirling his cue as he waited for his turn.

"Well, if someone was a little less distracted, we'd have you boys so far gone you'd tuck in your tails and head home." Blake tried to decide which ball to sink. This week his partner was the one off his game, checking his watch and cell phone constantly. "Leo, you got troubles? Other than the twenty we're ready to lose if you don't concentrate a little more?"

Leo grinned sheepishly. "Cari's supposed to get back into town tonight or tomorrow. I'm waiting for her call."

"Save us from the lovebirds. Leo, you and Cari are soooo sweet." Jesse turned and pulled a face at Blake and Joel.

Blake snorted. "Six ball, right-side pocket." He lined up the shot and sank the ball in one smooth, easy motion. Handing the cue to Leo, he went back to his beer.

He wasn't going to let Jesse know he really was tired. Sleep was hard to come by since he'd witnessed Jaxi in all her glory in the shower. His nights had gotten worse after she'd blown up at him at the community hall. He tossed and turned, hard and aching, all night long with no easy solution to his problem.

"You enjoying the guest cabin, Blake?" Joel kicked his legs freely as he sat on top of a nearby table, watching Leo take his shot.

Blake grunted.

"Guess Jaxi needed a little more room than the office space. What a gentleman you are to offer your bed." Jesse's eyes twinkled with mischief.

Blake flashed him a dirty look. Damn twins could poke all they wanted, but no way would he would confess he'd changed rooms because he didn't trust himself to be close to the girl and not make a move on her.

Hell, the way she'd acted in the shower, inviting him to touch her, he didn't trusted her to stay away from him. There was no use in begging for trouble.

Then there was the whole "Showdown at O.K. Corral" two nights ago. What a fucking nightmare. He hated that he'd hurt her, the expression in her eyes almost enough to make him reconsider, if only to be allowed to wipe away the pain.

He'd admit it. Jaxi had grown up. But he couldn't let her goad him into doing something she'd regret. She was too young to really know what she wanted for the long haul, and he was *not* having a one-night stand with her. The pain of rejection was for her own good, even though sticking to his guns choked something deep inside him.

"Course, staying in the cabin means you've got much more privacy if you need it." Joel jumped off the table with a whoop of delight. "Leo, you blew that shot. Our turn."

Joel and Jesse alternated in sinking balls, raising their score to seventy-five before they missed. Blake sipped his beer and glanced around, letting the familiar décor soothe his tired nerves.

On this side of the hall, people sat and talked, or played pool and relaxed. Next door, the music was louder, the dance floor wide and the bar open late. He and the boys were the only ones playing pool tonight, tucked into the back corner where it was quiet and private.

Blake was getting up for his turn when he saw her. Jaxi breezed in the doorway, pale blonde hair floating around her head.

"Sweet mercy, angel entering the room." Jesse breathed out the words in mock ecstasy.

She did look like an angel. For the past couple of weeks, Jaxi had worn plain jeans or jean shorts with cotton shirts. She'd pulled her hair into a sensible ponytail while she cooked and canned and worked around the house with his ma.

Tonight her sundress consisted of layers of flimsy material that lifted and floated in different directions as she sashayed forward. The clinging top left her smooth shoulders bare, the scooped neckline revealing deep cleavage of pearly pink skin. The fluttering layers of the skirt slid over her smooth legs, stopping well above her knees. The whole thing was cut from shades of yellow and gold, making her glow like a ray of sunshine.

Jesse rushed forward to greet her. Blake bit back a growl as his brother took her hand and placed it under his arm to escort her to their table, his lips tight to her ear as he spoke.

Jaxi's gaze flicked to Blake for a brief second before she laughed at Jesse, then turned to beam at Joel and Leo.

"Evening, boys. I was looking for Lindy but I've been told she's gone for the weekend. Mind if I join you instead?" Jaxi leaned in and kissed Leo's cheek, and Blake's arms jerked as he held himself back.

So much for a relaxing evening with the boys.

"Leo, I haven't seen you in forever. Where've you been hiding?" Jaxi stood close, her hands resting on Leo's arm. Blake turned away and retrieved his beer. At this rate he would need another one pretty damn quick.

"It's been busy at the shop lately. And you know, well, Cari and me..." Leo grinned at her. "I owe you one. Big time. Can I get you a drink?"

"Whoa there, stud," Jesse teased. "You've already got yourself a woman. I'll get Jaxi her drink. What'll you have, sweetheart?"

"Any you boys drinking draft tonight?"

"Joel and I are," Jesse volunteered.

"Can I join you?"

Jesse grinned from ear to ear and twirled her in his arms as if they were on the dance floor, snuggling her tight against his body. "I thought you'd never ask."

Jaxi slapped his shoulders as she laughed up at him. "Jesse, I swear. You've got the dirtiest mind. Get me a beer and get on with your game."

"Yes, ma'am." Jesse dropped a quick kiss on her nose before he let her go.

Blake stared at Jaxi. She was deliberately flirting with the twins and ignoring him, like she'd done since Wednesday. He couldn't believe she would taunt him. She wouldn't dare follow up on the challenge she'd thrown and fool around with the twins just to spite him.

Would she?

"Ma all right alone tonight?" Blake kicked himself even as the words escaped.

Jaxi did a slow rotation toward him, her face flushed. "No, Blake, she had a pounding headache, a pile of laundry to fold and just before I left I set a swarm of wasps loose in the house." She strode over and hopped up next to Joel on the table, her skirts flaring out to brush his thigh. Joel raised his eyebrows at his brothers, then took a long, slow look along the length of exposed leg next to him, smiling with appreciation.

"So. Now that we're all clear Blake is an ass, whose turn is it?" Leo didn't even try to hide his smirk.

Blake stepped forward. "Jaxi, I didn't mean I thought you'd—"

"You planning on dancing later?" Jaxi leaned a little closer to Joel, her left breast rubbing his arm as she ignored Blake.

"If you need a partner."

Jaxi slipped her fingers into his and winked at Jesse hovering on her other side. "Your ma and dad went to visit friends and told me they didn't need me until tomorrow morning. I guess I have some time to kill."

Blake felt like shit as he turned back to the table.

Although he'd decided it was best for her to not be with him, the decision wasn't sitting easy. Watching her with the twins hurt worse than he thought possible. He wanted to be the one holding her hand and whispering in her ear. Taking her close against him on the dance floor and feeling her soft skin rub every inch of his body.

"Nine ball, corner pocket."

Blake and Leo brought the score to eighty-seven before they missed. It was an exquisite form of torture for Blake as he moved around the table taking shots. Every now and then he'd sight his cue in Jaxi's direction, see Joel's arm casually tucked behind her back. Jesse sat on her other side, their thighs tight together, his fingers draped over both their legs. She was sandwiched between them just like Joel had described days ago, and Blake's temper rose.

He had told them to stay away from her. Warned them not to get too close in private, let alone in public. Joel met his eye with a challenge that was about far more than pool as he stepped to the table, and the twins quickly took their score over one hundred to win.

"I guess that means we keep the record for another week, right, old-timers?" Jesse held his hand toward Leo and Blake. Leo slapped a twenty into his palm.

"We have time for another game," Blake suggested. Anything to keep the twins from taking Jaxi into the dancehall before he decided what he was going to do. In spite of all his good intentions, there was a bitter taste in his mouth.

Jesse gave him a grin that said it all. "Well, that's up to Jaxi. What do you say, sweetheart, can you wait a little longer for your dance?"

Jaxi wiggled her way off the table, letting Joel ease her to the ground. "You go ahead and play another round. I'll join you in a few minutes."

Dead silence filled the area as they all paused to watch her hips sway as she headed for the ladies' room, the layers of her skirt flaring around her legs like windblown leaves.

Leo whistled, long and low. "Sweet. That woman is one hot piece of action waiting to happen." He turned back to the brothers, his face innocent and blank. "So, do I get to watch a fight to see which one of you takes her home tonight?"

Jesse and Joel snickered, their dark blond heads shaking. "We're all taking her home. She's staying with us to help our ma."

Leo flipped a hand at him. "I know that, and that's not what I asked. She's been waiting for one of you Six Pack boys for as long as I've known her. I just can't figure which one. Spill."

Blake glared a warning at the twins. "What do you mean, waiting for one of us?"

Leo shrugged. "I noticed it more after Cari said something to me once. Jaxi's willing to flirt with the twins, but she's got her eyes all over you, Blake. The way the woman watches you I'd think you'd feel her burning a hole in your backside." Leo examined Blake's face closely. "You had no idea, did you? Maybe you need to spend a little less time in the fields and a little more time around people. Jaxi's got plans, and she's moving on them. I can hardly wait to see how this one shakes down."

Jaxi returned by the time they'd racked the balls, and Leo got ready to take the first shot.

"Playing one hundred again?" she asked.

"It's our favourite way to embarrass the old folks," Joel taunted.

Jaxi's gaze raked Blake from top to bottom. He stiffened at the blatant appraisal, the sexual gleam she didn't even try to hide. "Pretty nice looking for old folks." She turned to Jesse. "I haven't seen you play Challenge lately. Why don't you do a round of it for me?"

"Challenge?" Leo whispered to Blake.

What was the minx up to? Challenge was usually played with mixed teams and it was definitely a flirting game. Downright foreplay at times. Jaxi tucked her cell phone away in her purse and shimmied back onto the table.

"Challenge sounds fine to us," Joel called. "We can beat you faster than in a normal game since you'll be too embarrassed to sink any balls."

Leo shrugged. "I'm game." He pointed a finger at Jaxi. "I don't know what you're doing, little lady, but I'll play along this time. You got Cari to give me another chance, and I can put up with a little tomfoolery for your sake."

Jaxi winked at him and sat back to watch.

The twins won the break, and Blake tried to remember a game challenge that wasn't too raunchy. He wasn't interested in getting up close and personal with Leo or his brothers. This had to be the most insane suggestion ever.

"First ten points, consecutive pockets starting with far right."

Jesse hooted. "You worried about making us blush, big brother?"

Bastard. "Just shoot."

Jesse and Joel took their turns, managing to sink eight balls in a row into the appropriate pockets before missing. Blake and Leo took over and put away two more before Jesse cleared his throat to announce the next challenge.

"Triple Play."

"Hell, Jesse, you're kidding," Leo complained. "Do I need to worry about why you want to slip between me and Blake while we shoot?"

Jesse shook his head. "Not me. I figured we could talk Jaxi into helping us." He turned and held a hand to the girl. "What do you think, sweetheart? Run a little interference for us?"

Blake's heartbeat increased as Jaxi took the hand offered her and smiled sweetly at Jesse. The boy had the guts to clasp her by the waist and slowly lower her to the ground, letting their bodies rub together on the way.

Jaxi propelled herself back from Jesse's arms with a wink. "I'm in, but I'm supposed to start with the other team. Troublemaker." She patted Jesse's cheek and turned toward Blake, her eyes flashing. "Unless you'd rather give up right now and admit defeat. I never took you for a quitter, but I guess you can never tell when things will get too hot for a person to handle."

Blake shoved down his anger. She wanted to play with fire, did she? He was nearly ready to burn through her teasing and take her on the table, right in front of the whole world, if she didn't back off. Damn the consequences.

He turned away to examine the table for a sinkable shot. "Twelve in the side pocket, Leo." His partner nodded and eyeballed the line before placing his hand on the table for Blake to rest the cue on. Leo twisted his body far to the side, leaving plenty of room for Blake to make the shot using only one hand.

Except Triple Play meant Jaxi had to be between him and Leo. Touching them both at the same time. Blake threw Jesse an evil look, and a roar of laughter blasted back at him.

"I did shower recently," Jaxi said, moving in close.

Bloody hell. Don't talk about showers right now.

Blake wrapped an arm around her and brought her to his side. She slid her arms around to his back and clung tightly as he leaned over the table, positioned the cue on Leo's outstretched hand and took the shot.

Jaxi's sweet scent rose around them, her breath hot on his neck as he stood. Tension built in his gut, not only from the feel of her against his body. Nine more balls to sink before they went to the next challenge, and he would go insane if he had to watch his little brothers spoon Jaxi between the two of them.

Leo picked a shot and Blake set up the cradle. Instead of hugging onto Leo, Jaxi slid close to Blake again, resting against his chest, her breasts compressed against him, swelling to the top of the scooped neck of her dress. Blake bit back a groan.

"You got troubles, Blake?" Jaxi whispered in his ear. She licked him, her hot little tongue slipping into his ear, making his whole body jerk in reaction.

"Hell, Blake, stay still," Leo complained. The ball bounced sideways, shy of the pocket, and rolled to a stop.

"Our turn for a bit. Come here, sweetheart, and give me some sugar." Jesse checked Blake for a reaction before bussing Jaxi on the lips.

Blake glared daggers at his little brother.

Joel got into position, kneeling with one leg up, his arm resting casually on the table to his side. "Ride side saddle if you want."

Jaxi flicked another glance at Blake, then strolled forward confidently. "Side saddle is for cowards."

She stepped on either side of his leg and lowered herself to straddle him, her skirt lifting to expose more of her long limbs. Blake gritted his teeth as Joel pulled her in tight, squeezing their bodies close as she slid over him. Jaxi made a soft sound of pleasure, her expression nowhere near as confident as only moments before. She bit her lower lip, and Jesse swore, folding his body over them to sink the shot. He lifted her and got ready for the next shot.

Blake drained his beer and tried not to watch as Jaxi and Jesse and Joel wrapped around each other for another six shots. Each time it took longer to arrange the positioning. Jesse slid his hands over Jaxi thoroughly as he prepared, pulling her tighter to himself or pushing her against Joel as he pretended to adjust for line. Jaxi's face grew flushed, her heartbeat visible in the hollow of her neck, her breathing more and more rapid. Her eyes were huge, her gaze following Blake everywhere.

Blake died a little with every touch of his brothers' hands on Jaxi. Every time their mouths brushed her skin, every time their hips and torsos pressed together.

He faced the wall and clenched his fists tight. He was going to stalk out the door or he was going to kill someone. Or some two.

Jaxi bit back a cry, breathless and low.

"Holy shit," Leo muttered.

Blake turned back to see Joel had Jaxi draped over his arm, bent forward, as he pressed against her back to take a shot off Jesse's shoulder. Joel moved slowly, slipping the pool cue back as if he needed more time. He bent his mouth to Jaxi's ear and whispered something while he caressed her breast with his free hand. She gasped and arched under him.

Both of Jesse's hands were free to slide along the long legs spread in front of where he knelt on the ground. One flowed up her leg, under her dress, then over her ass. The other hand wasn't visible but Blake could imagine what Jesse was doing as the bastard stared into Jaxi's flushed face, his eyes wild as he watched her tremble under his touch.

Blake saw red. The blood rushing through him heated to boiling as his endurance failed. "Enough!"

The sensual dance fell apart. Joel stood slowly, keeping Jaxi in his arms as he backed them away from where Jesse knelt, head bowed, breathing uneven, fists pressed hard on his thighs. He rose unsteadily to his feet, his eyes glazed as he fought for control. Lifting his fingers to his mouth, Jesse's blue eyes riveted on Jaxi.

Leo's phone rang.

He swore and turned away to answer it, retreating to the front room and leaving the three brothers alone with Jaxi.

The only sound was the dull beat of the music echoing from the far side of the wall. Blake focused on the one undeniable truth before him. In the past five minutes something had changed, and there was no going back. Either he stepped up or he stepped aside.

Did he want her?

Damn, he wanted her so bad he had to restrain himself from tossing her over his shoulder like a caveman and hightailing out to his truck for a little action in the back. Or forget even making it to the truck, he'd slip them into the back room and fuck her against the wall, hard and fast, until they both made more of those noises of pleasure she was so good at producing. His cock was rock hard from watching her with his brothers, and every breath he took hurt.

But it was her expression that threatened to bring him to his knees. She'd been in Joel's arms, Jesse's hand on her body, but she stared at Blake as if he was the one who had just rocked her world.

The difference in their ages, her having been Travis's girlfriend, being a big-brother figure when he wanted much more—all the issues haunting him faded to insignificance in light of how much he needed her.

Why in the hell had he kept them apart?

He took a step toward her. Her hair lay tousled around her face, wisps of curls stuck in the air in spots. A trickle of sweat ran down her neck, past her collarbone. She breathed hard, her eyes glittering grey stars shining straight into his soul.

"Blake?"

Her voice trembled.

She bit her lower lip again and Blake drew in a harsh breath. He didn't step toward her, frozen by the sight of Jesse's fingers trailing along her arm, by Joel leaning in close to her other side and nuzzling her neck.

"So, you decided?" Jesse whispered. "Are we taking Jaxi home or are you? Or all of us? Because it's high time this headed somewhere a little more private."

Blake damned himself for waiting, for giving the twins a chance to touch her and make her want them. Now he couldn't rip her from their arms.

She had to choose.

He flicked his head to the side. The twins stepped back a pace, leaving Jaxi standing in the middle of their circle. She swayed as her legs supported her full weight alone for the first time since the start of the game.

"Jaxi, who..." He hesitated. He wasn't going to beg, but he wanted her to know what he was asking. This wasn't just about right here and right now. He caressed her cheek with his hand. "You offered me something pretty special the other night and I turned you down."

Jesse and Joel exchanged quick looks.

"I wasn't sure what the right thing to do was, I'll admit it. But I'm not uncertain anymore. If you still want me."

He was going to drown in her eyes. The tip of her tongue slipped out and wet her lips. Jaxi narrowed her eyes, and her voice dropped to a whisper. Soft and intimate, just for his ears.

"You still think you're too old for me, Blake Coleman? Because I don't want someone who's going to be all careful and delicate with me when what you want is a woman to make love with—"

He crushed her to him, slanting his mouth over hers to taste her lips for the first time. Sweet honey and hops lingered on her tongue, but the overwhelming flavor was Jaxi and nothing else. Blake ate at her mouth hungrily, lifting her body to his to mold her close, his fingers cradling the cheeks of her ass as he tried to wrap her around him more intimately. Jaxi had her fingers in his hair, keeping them so tight together that if he needed to breathe it was going to have to be through her. He barely stopped from ripping her clothes off. But as much as he wanted to touch her everywhere, a small part of his mind remembered they were in a public place.

A very small part.

He wrenched his mouth from hers and dropped his head to her shoulder. Somehow they'd crossed the room until they were against the pool table. Jaxi's hips rested on the edge of the green felt, legs spread wide to allow Blake to fit between, snug against her crotch. The heat of her sex burned through the thin fabric of her dress and his denim jeans, and Blake took a deep breath and fought for control.

"You two want us to create a road block at the door or you going to make it home okay?" Joel's quiet question hung in the air.

Jaxi squirmed.

"What?" Blake asked.

She pulled him close to whisper in his ear. "You don't know how tempted I am to say 'road block' right now."

He swallowed hard. "I'm not taking you for the first time on a pool table, Slick."

104

"How about the sixth? Or tenth? Promise me sometime we can do it on a pool table—"

Blake dragged her off the table and into his arms. "You keep talking like that, and we won't make it anywhere but the parking lot."

Chapter Ten

Blake carried her out the door of the hall. A couple of wolf whistles echoed in their direction, and Jaxi tucked her face farther into the crook of his neck. She was finally in his arms, where she'd longed to be, but his touch was new enough she wanted their relationship to remain private.

By morning the whole town would know. Was Blake ready?

"You sure about this? You take me back inside, and we can pretend this was a joke. We can keep it a secret for a bit. Otherwise everyone will talk."

She couldn't believe she'd actually said that. Thank God, listening to her suggestions seemed to be the farthest thing from his mind. He kissed her again, his hands possessive on her body as he lowered her then drew their hips together intimately, pressing his rigid cock against the softness of her belly. His tongue swept over her teeth, tasting and teasing, as he leaned her back against the side of his truck, trapping her between the unyielding metal and the solid length of his body.

Jaxi's head was spinning before he drew back, his eyes dark with arousal. "This is no joke, and I don't give a damn who knows I'm taking you home with me tonight. Unless you tell me right now you don't want me, I plan on being buried as deep as possible in you, as soon as I can, and they could sell tickets for all I care."

"I want you. I've always wanted you," Jaxi gasped.

Blake closed his eyes for a second before he cupped her face in his hands. "Then you need to stop fussing. You didn't seem worried about people watching you when it was the twins who were doing the touching. I guess maybe I need to ask you the same thing you asked me. Am I too old for you? Are you able to offer me everything I need? 'Cause I don't want a shy little thing in my bed, or someone who's worried about what other people will say. In fact, I want a woman who's not afraid to seduce me right under other people's noses, like I saw the other day in the shower. Someone who'll wear a sexy dress and maybe even leave her panties behind so I can touch her anytime and anywhere I want. Someone who can handle me as hard and as often as I need. So you look at me with those big eyes of yours and you tell me. Are you able to give me everything I need?"

Blake breathed hard, his chest rising and falling fast, his hands on her strong and firm. She'd watched him for many years, seen him in many different moods. She'd never seen him like he was tonight.

Raw. Needy.

All male.

Everything she'd longed for.

She reached to grab one of his hands and pulled it to her lips, staring into his eyes as she kissed his palm. Without a word she tugged until his strong hand rested between her legs, cupping her mound. Slowly, inch-by-inch, she wiggled up the filmy layers of her skirt until they slipped from under his hand.

And his fingers touched the soft curls of her body.

Their eyes were still connected the moment he realized she was naked under her dress. The heat that flashed was enough to send a wave of desire through her body, causing a flood of liquid to slip over his fingers.

"Damn it, Slick, I'm not going to last thirty seconds with you, am I?"

Her head fell back against the window as he touched her, his thick, work-toughened fingers gently caressing her labia. He separated her and pressed in a circle over the tight nub at the apex of her mound. Blake touched his lips to the side of her neck, nipped at the tendon there, then soothed it with a sweep of his tongue. He leaned in close, speaking just above a whisper.

"I was going to drive you straight home, but before we leave I think you owe me something. You owe me for letting Jesse and Joel touch you and bring you pleasure in front of my eyes. So we're going to stay right here until you drop some more sweet honey on my fingers and you make more of those sweet sounds from your lips. You're going to let me watch you come apart, and it will be my hand that takes you there."

His mouth descended again—hot and needy, demanding and incessant. He kissed her as his fingers stroked, circled, teased. Pressure built through her core, an uneasy balance of pleasurable tension and tingling ache. Blake rubbed her clit while his tongue delved into her mouth, twisting her emotions even as his hand twisted her senses into overload.

He pressed one long finger deep, swallowing the gasp of pleasure that escaped from her lips.

They stood in the shadows on the side of the parking lot, lights flicking past from the occasional vehicle. The glare of headlights faded to nothing as Blake continued, slow and even, to press into her sheath. She opened her legs wider, instinctively trying to ease his passage, attempting to let him farther into her aching core. The warm August air gusted around them, and heat flowed over her skin as his fingers continued to caress, the heel of his hand unwavering against her throbbing clit.

He matched the motion of his tongue and finger, his other hand supporting her neck to let him angle her exactly how he wanted. He rubbed their bodies together, friction adding to the heat between them.

Her core tightened, her breasts grew hot and aching as they pressed against his hard chest. Moisture fell from her body to slide along her thighs. Still he continued, his erection against her leg proof of how much it affected him to touch her, to feel her response.

Blake bit her lips, dragging her body closer as he sped the pace of his hand and hips. Jaxi cried out as the increase in stimulation possessed her, swept around her, swept over her, and propelled her over the edge. His kisses grew more desperate as he rocked against her a few more times, then clutched her hard. Their harsh breathing echoed off the parked cars around them.

Blake cradled her until she stopped shaking.

"Damn it, I haven't come in my jeans since I was in tenth grade." His lips brushed her temple, light and gentle, and Jaxi took a deep breath and tried to stop the world from spinning.

Sweet sounds of the night, the faint throb of the music from the bar, voices in the distance—all echoed loudly in her ears until the blood pounding through her slowed.

"You got your car keys?" Blake asked quietly.

"In my purse. You want me to meet you at home?"

"No way you're getting away that easy. You're coming with me. I've got your car covered. Keys."

Jaxi slipped her purse from her shoulder and dug into it. She passed her keychain to him, wondering what he planned to do with her vehicle. Blake turned, searching the shadows. He threw her keys with a sudden snap, and Jaxi bit her lip as Jesse stepped forward and caught them in mid-air.

Joel appeared next to him and the four stared at each other for a moment. Jaxi swallowed hard. The twins must have been watching the whole time, but she couldn't find anywhere in her that was distressed.

Turned on more than she imagined possible, but not upset.

Joel nodded once and moved away, fading like a ghost into the darkness. Jesse hesitated a moment longer. His blue eyes flicked between her and Blake before he lifted his fingers and blew her a kiss. Then he too disappeared.

She shivered even as a shot of desire raced through her. The night was growing hotter and hotter, and she had a good idea where the next step would lead.

Blake turned her to face him, cupping her chin in his hand. "You mad at me for letting them see you're mine?"

Jaxi linked her arms around his neck and lifted her mouth. She swept one leg up the back of his thigh as far as she could lift, pressing hard against him. When they separated, she went for broke. There was no way she wanted to keep this a secret any longer than she already had. "You mad they helped set you up? To force you to acknowledge how much you wanted me?"

Blake froze. For a moment, he didn't respond.

"You planned it? The game, the flirting?"

Jaxi looked away for a second before she drew in her courage and stared him down. "Yeah, I set it up, but it didn't work as planned. Leo was supposed to get called away, and I was going to end up your partner for the game of Challenge. But Leo was still there and Jesse pulled a fast one calling Triple

110

Play. I thought to hell with it, hoping it would shake you enough you'd come to your senses and realize you wanted me."

Blake shook his head slowly. "Wanting you has never been the problem." He yanked open the truck door and helped her in the driver side, pulling her hip back against his when she would have scooted to the passenger side.

He looked at her hard for a minute. "You're one dangerous woman, Jaxi."

She waited, nearly unable to breathe.

He chuckled.

All her tension released in one fell swoop. He could have been angry, getting set up like that. Heck, he could have been annoyed with Jesse and Joel for being more than willing to play along and pushing it too far.

"You planned any more games for tonight? Anything I need to know about before we go home?"

Jaxi shook her head.

"Good, I'm in charge of the evening from here on. No twins popping in and out, no games of chance." Blake reversed out of the lot and was on the street faster than she thought possible. "No worrying about what the ladies at the salon will say tomorrow. No worrying about who's too old and who's too young."

The streets of town sped past. The heat of his thigh next to hers, the gentle bumping of her body against his side, even the scent of his skin in the cab of the truck—all of it exactly what she'd been longing for. Then they were on the gravel, headed down the side roads that would bring them to the Coleman spread. Blake's hand lay on her thigh, his thumb tracing small circles as he inched her skirt farther up.

"You always traipse round with no panties, Slick? Or was that just luck back there?"

Jaxi sucked in air as Blake exposed her bare crotch. "I don't usually, but since I'd planned..."

"Right, the plan." He brushed his knuckles over her curls. "Slide down a little. I want to see better."

Jaxi flicked a glance at his face. He watched the road, a smile curving the corner of his mouth. She wiggled her hips lower and let the fabric of her dress ride up until her lower body was completely visible.

Blake hummed in approval. "Now that's a nice sight. But you don't look too comfy, all scrunched up like that. Maybe you'd better shuck the dress altogether." His gaze had returned to the road while his hand stroked the tops of her thighs like a soft wind caressing over the wheat field.

She slipped off her seat belt and tugged the light fabric over her head in one motion. She flushed red-hot, determined to follow Blake's instructions.

He took the corner onto the long driveway that led to the dark and quiet ranch house before slowing the truck to a stop. He turned to look at Jaxi, his gaze gliding over her body as intimate as the touch of a hand. Her nipples tightened. She knew what he saw. The folds of her body still wet from earlier, her naked breasts swollen with need. Blake didn't speak. He just looked for a good long time before he put the truck back in gear and drove the final distance to the house.

"You're a pretty little thing, you know that, Jaxi? Soft everywhere." Blake's hand covered her mound possessively, cradling her. "Tell me what you like. How you want to be touched so you feel real good. You enjoy kisses down here? Such a pretty little bit of candy for a man to lick and suck."

She drew in a breath. "No one's ever..."

He swore and heat flushed her body, starting from where his hand held her like a prize. He pulled in beside the cabin and took away his hand to slam the shift into park. He took a deep breath through his nose and let it out slowly.

"Jaxi, I'm wondering what you're doing because I'm getting a tad confused by the signals you're sending. I'm going to carry you inside, and you think about what you need to tell me when we get there. Just so there are no more surprises."

Blake jerked open his door but he was careful as he tugged Jaxi after him. Her naked body was cradled in his arms as he strode to the cabin, his expression like thunderclouds ready to roll.

She was in a pile of trouble from the looks of things.

Chapter Eleven

He kicked open the door and deposited her on the bed. Stepping back, he took a seat in one of the chairs set by the small table in the corner. His things were neatly tucked away, except for the pile of clean laundry she'd brought in after supper.

He watched, unblinking.

Jaxi forced herself to sit straight as Blake stared. His gaze ate her up, one inch of skin at a time, from top to the bottom before he spoke.

"We're taking this all the way, so you'd better tell me what you know and what you've been holding back." He leaned forward, elbows resting on his knees, a smoky smile building on his face that made her shiver with anticipation. "Or maybe we'll turn it into a little puzzle for me to solve, since you enjoy games."

He yanked off his boots and tossed them to the side. He stood and unbuckled his belt. She licked her suddenly dry lips, and Blake chuckled. "See, that's what I'm talking about. I think you're a whole lot more innocent than you've been trying to let on. Then you go and do something like that, all sex kitten and wanton, and you tie my brain in knots. Now I'm going to get naked 'cause you made me lose all control back there in the parking lot, and I'm not sitting around in wet jeans anymore."

Jaxi wiggled up to a kneeling position, her face burning with heat.

He laughed. "Look at you. Flushed and eager. I know damn well you've already seen me naked, so don't you turn away or try to get shy."

He popped open the button on his jeans, and her heart beat faster.

"Can I help?" She couldn't take her gaze off his hands as he peeled back the zipper and opened his jeans.

"Not this time. You touch me, and we'll be rushing places you're not ready for. So, no man's ever kissed your pussy?"

He dropped his jeans. His boxer briefs were wet, a dark patch showing against the front.

"Hey, Slick."

Jaxi dragged her gaze back to his face with effort.

"Damn, you've got the biggest eyes. You going to tell me what I need to know?" He unbuttoned his shirt slowly, the rustle of fabric loud in the quiet room. He pulled it off and grasped the bottom of his T-shirt, his hard abs appearing bit by bit as he lifted the material over his head.

He stripped off his boxers and then, glory be, sat naked in the chair, his muscles shifting as he leaned back to get comfortable and let her look him over. Jaxi had enjoyed her little voyeur trip the other day, but it was nothing compared to gazing at Blake Coleman, gloriously naked, three feet away from her. She admired the muscles in his arms, on his chest, the ridges of his abdomen, the firm strength of his thighs. All there while he showed himself off like a prize bull.

His cock rose from his lap, tapping toward the six-pack of his abdomen. Jaxi could barely breathe for wanting to touch.

To taste.

Blake rose to his feet and prowled his way to the bed, his cock aimed like an arrow at her. She scooted backward, never taking her gaze off him, as he dropped to his knees and crawled toward her.

"Lay on the bed, hands by your sides."

A thrill shot through her at the tone in his voice. She'd suspected being ordered around by him would turn her on. She lay back and pressed her palms to the quilt.

Blake suspended his body over hers, his legs straddling her knees. He was far enough away the heat of his body was a soft caress, a mere hint of energy radiating toward her.

He lowered a hand to touch her body. One finger.

Over her lips.

"You've kissed a few boys, haven't you?"

"Not many. But yeah, I've been kissed."

His chuckle echoed in the hushed room. "You've kissed all my brothers from what I heard."

Jaxi flicked her tongue against his fingertip as he traced her lips again and again. "I kissed them or they kissed me. That's all. No one else."

Blake's mouth descended slowly, brushing her mouth with a butterfly stroke. "I'm the only Coleman you're going to kiss from here on, understand?"

Jaxi strained upward, trying to regain his lips from where they hovered inches above hers.

"Not until you say it. Your mouth is mine. Kisses only for me."

She was going to die if she didn't get his mouth on hers now. "Yours. Only for you."

Blake gave no room for retreat as he demanded a response, feasting, licking and sucking until she was left utterly
116

breathless. Her hands rose to his neck, slicking through his short hair before he jerked back.

"Hands to the bed, I'm not done with my questions."

Jaxi dragged her nails over his back as she dropped her arms.

"You touch me and I stop. Now, let's see." His finger was back again, tracing from her mouth, over the curve of her chin, down her neck. She shivered as he drew the fingertip over her breast, circling the tight peak lazily. "Such beautiful breasts. I saw them in the shower the other day, all wet and glistening, and I wanted to pluck these juicy tips like ripe berries. Tell me, who's touched your breasts? Who's sucked these pretty things with their mouths and made you squirm?"

Jaxi arched up, trying to get him to connect with more than her nipple. He continued his slow assault, the heat in his touch melting through her defenses.

"Couple boys touched me. Travis with his mouth. Jesse and Joel tonight with their hands over my dress."

"Damn, my brothers have gotten more of you than they're ever going to get again." He lowered his head and licked the tip of her nipple. "Mine. These beauties are mine. Mine to hold and caress, mine to nibble and bite and—"

"Yours. Oh, please, put your mouth on me now," she sobbed.

Blake covered her with his hand, smoothed her skin, dragging his palm over the rigid peak as he caressed her. He lapped at her other nipple, sucking it into his mouth as his fingers rolled over her belly to her lower lips.

"You tell me who's touched this pretty pussy. You said no one's kissed you there. Who's had their hands on you, bringing you pleasure, besides me and Jesse?"

"Damn it, stop with the questions and give me what I need." Jaxi arched hard, thrusting her hips against his hand. She was on fire, and he was keeping her at such a steady burn she was liable to pass out from need.

He lowered his body on top of hers, thigh to thigh, his cock hard on top of her curls and stomach, hot fluid painting her belly. He increased their body contact and the weight pressed her into the bed so slowly every inch of his skin heated her to the melting point.

"You've never let anyone inside, have you? You don't know what it's going to feel like to have my cock press you apart, stretch you wide while you squeeze me tight. You don't know how good it'll feel when I pump into you, hard and fast, and fill you up."

Blake rocked his hips in short strokes, rubbing his shaft over her aching clit as she gasped and tried to press back for more. He stilled and she cried in loss. She wanted it all.

"No one's ever made love to me." She pulled her legs apart and sighed as he settled more firmly, his cock nestled tight against her aching core.

"Tell me why you're still a virgin, Slick. It ain't because you've never been asked."

Jaxi hesitated, then simply told the truth.

"I wanted you. And you never asked until now."

Blake dragged himself down her body, panting as he fought to maintain control. His forbidden fantasies, all the things he'd longed for, were coming true. His body sang with pleasure, his mind barely able to comprehend this was really happening. She was the most beautiful thing he'd ever seen, and in moments, she'd be all his. Not shared with his brothers like the stolen kisses of youth.

Just sweet, ripe fruit—mature pleasure shared between a man and woman.

He wouldn't last much longer. As much as he wanted to nibble every inch of her skin, as much as he needed to suck those firm breasts, he needed to be inside her more.

He wasn't going to do that until she was good and ready for him.

Blake pressed her legs farther apart with his shoulders and stared at her swollen lips peeking through the blonde curls. Moisture beaded there, a hot, sweet aroma rising to his nose. He used one finger to gently open her, and the pink folds of her labia bloomed in front of him.

He lowered his mouth and licked, tasting her cream, covering her with the warmth of his mouth as his tongue slicked up the other side. Jaxi made little noises of pleasure, her hips moving with her excitement, and he pressed one hand across her hips to lock her in place on the bed.

Blake swept over her again, concentrating on lapping every inch of smooth skin inside and out of the soft petals of her lips. He thrust his tongue into her core as far as it would go. Her body responded like he'd blown on coals, heat pouring from her as she cried out.

He needed two hands to restrain her. The taste of her, the scent of her passion overwhelmed him, and he lifted her hips into the air, hauling her closer to his mouth to feast easier. Blake dragged his tongue hard over her clit, and the convulsion that shook her body nearly ripped her from his grasp. He did it again, laving the length of her wet slit harder and faster until Jaxi screamed, and her core pulsed in waves with her orgasm.

Rising over her, he pressed his erection against her scalding heat. He rocked carefully, each motion spreading her cream and making the length of his shaft ready for her. When

119

she protested, he changed angles, slipping the head of his cock between her folds, moving inward slowly until she froze.

Blake dropped his mouth to hers and bit her lip, flicking his tongue against her mouth until she opened. As she responded to his kiss, he pulled back his hips, then thrust to bury himself deep.

Jaxi gasped into his mouth, her body gone tense. Blake locked their hips in place, forcing himself to wait until she relaxed and eased around his girth. He kissed her softly, licking and nibbling until she squirmed under him.

"Alright?"

"Damn, you've split me in two. It feels, oh hell, it feels good but..."

"Oh, Slick, you're amazing. Just wait, I'm going to move. Nice and slow."

He watched her closely as he withdrew a short way and eased back in. He grinned as her eyes rolled back in her head and she moaned.

"Oh yeah, that feels better. Do it again."

Blake kissed her as he rocked in and out slowly, dragging his body over her as he memorized the taste of her lips, the feel of her tongue tangling with his.

"Bend your legs, open to me a little more."

She shifted, and on the next thrust, the crown of his shaft bumped her inside. She let out a squeak, but the way she tried to open even wider let him know she wasn't opposed to the sensation.

He finally noticed she still clutched the quilt with a death hold and he chuckled. "You can touch me if you want."

Jaxi instantly wrapped her arms around him and helped pull him deeper. "I wasn't going to take a chance and have you stop. More, I need more."

She lifted her hips toward him a couple of inches, speeding his movements.

He was only going slowly for her sake. On the next thrust he went a little harder, forcing her into the bed. One hand slipped between their bodies, as he looked to step up her pleasure quicker. He wanted to feel her come, to feel her body welcome him in and delight in him. Wet and ready, he stroked her clit as he pumped his hips faster. She squeezed him, her passage slick with moisture but tight around him as his cock rubbed again and again.

Under him Jaxi shook, her breath coming in short, tight pants. Her wide eyes stared at him as she took his thrusts willingly, eagerly. She tightened around him and cried out, waves of pressure squeezing around his shaft. He pumped twice more, releasing his control to explode into her hot depths.

It was like coming home. Locked together, hearts pounding wildly, Blake had never felt such a sense of belonging. Such a feeling of being right where he needed to be. He stared into her pleasure-glazed eyes and leaned down to kiss her again.

He barely managed to roll to the side to avoid crushing her, their bodies still tangled together intimately as they stroked each other, unable to stop touching. Blake nudged her head back to get at her mouth. He wanted more of her taste, the feel of her gentling under his mouth.

The reality of loving her beat all the fantasies he'd ever had.

He would be ready to go again if he kept this up, and it was too soon for her to handle him yet. Distraction needed—he had to care for her. He gave her one last kiss before pulling away to get a washcloth.

She was all soft and relaxed when he returned, lying on the surface of the quilt with her arms back by her sides, one leg bent. As he knelt beside her, touching her carefully, the realization struck like a brick wall.

He'd taken her without a condom.

Every pass of the cloth he made as carefully as possible, a strange fog filling his mind. The cloth was dropped to the floor, then he drew her back into his arms, brain-fuddled and blood roaring in his ears.

He'd never done that before. Never even been tempted. Every time he'd been with a woman, he'd sheathed up early with no questions asked, no matter if she said she was protected. He was clean, but...

Fuck.

Jaxi curled in tighter to his side, her warmth scorching his body as his guilty conscience seared his mind.

Blake dropped another kiss on the top of her head as he struggled out of post-coital mindlessness into what-the-hell-had-they-just-done territory. And why.

It wasn't the kind of mistake he would make. He stared at the ceiling, wondering if he'd done it on purpose. On some level, had he wanted to mark her permanently as his, make sure this wasn't a one-time deal?

There was nothing more permanent than a baby.

Jaxi laughed softly in his arms and jostled him, her bright smile fading as she caught a glimpse of his face.

"What's wrong?"

"Nothing wrong, but..." He tried to sound gentle and caring, but he was afraid the question came out a little scared. "You on the pill?"

She looked confused for a minute before her lashes dropped and hid her eyes from his view. "Oh, damn. I didn't even think about that."

He kissed her cheek, tried to convey his emotions with the action since the words were stuck in his throat. Hell, the words were stuck in his brain—he didn't quite know what he was even thinking.

Jaxi wiggled back and he reluctantly released her.

"Are you going to flip out on me? You regret making love and now you're going to head for the hills?" Her eyes had filled with moisture, and Blake's heart cracked at the hurt he'd unwittingly caused.

"I ain't going anywhere, Slick. I know what I feel inside. I just don't want you to think you have to agree to anything because I made a mistake."

She shivered as she sat up.

"I hate that word. Mistake. Don't you ever use that word again, Blake Coleman. If we made a baby right now, it's no mistake. Even if we had used a condom, I could get pregnant."

Her indignation was stronger than he'd expected. "What you telling me?"

She blushed. Hard. Harder than he'd ever seen. Then she lifted her chin and stared him down as she spoke.

"You want me to spell it out for you? I hear you say my kisses are all yours, and my body is all yours, and I tell you no one's ever made love to me before because I was waiting for you. If you weren't thinking about forever, Blake, fine. But I was. That's why I almost don't care that we didn't use a condom, and why if...hell, if I had my way we'd be making love again in about two minutes, condom or no. 'Cause even if it scares you I've got to tell you—I've been thinking about you and loving and forever. I've been thinking about it for a long time."

123

Blake stared at her, all bold as brass as she sat naked at the foot of the bed.

Damn, she was glorious.

He reached and enveloped her in his arms. Tried to ease the tension in her shoulders, relax the tightness from her body with pets and caresses and whispers against her skin. He slid her over him, letting her weight cover him with heat and silky pleasure. He took her face between his hands and kissed her tenderly on the eyelids. Used his lips to brush away the tears that hung there.

Had he thought about forever? He'd wanted her forever, and she felt right in his arms. A part of his heart had always belonged to her. He kissed her mouth, simple and soft, before whispering over her cheek.

"You make me feel the biggest fool, Slick, 'cause you're braver than anyone I know. I can tell you with my body how I feel about you, but saying the words seems mighty hard."

He brushed his hands down her back, stroking and soothing. He rolled them to their sides and kissed her cheeks, feathered his fingers over her collarbone, tracing the delicate lines. Her eyes still showed hurt, but a trace of something else lit the corners. Hope? This was as good a time as any. He smiled at her.

A loud pounding on the door of the cabin jerked him from where he was headed.

"I'm going to kill them, whoever it is." Blake dragged himself away from her warmth and stumbled to the door. He yanked the door open a crack, using his body to shield the cabin from prying eyes.

Joel's white face filled his gaze. "I'm damn sorry for interrupting, but we just got word. Mama and Daddy collided with a moose on their way home tonight. The truck's a wreck, and they've been taken to the hospital in Red Deer."

Chapter Twelve

Blake sat in the easy chair in his father's hospital room, listening to the gentle sound of breathing. Jaxi lay curled up in his lap, her warm breath drifting over his neck, bosom pressed against his arm.

They'd checked in on his ma first. The nurses told them with the pain medication it was unlikely Marion would wake before morning. His dad, however, would be woken soon to monitor him for a concussion.

Blake was grateful neither of them had been more seriously hurt. Although his ma was going to be right ticked when she heard the news.

As he waited for his dad to wake, Blake looked at the bit of woman in his arms. Soft, yet strong, and definitely all woman. He couldn't believe she was here. After denying them both for so long, it felt right to have her warmth penetrating all the way through to his heart. Even if a bit of him was scared shitless they'd made love unprotected.

"Blake?" His dad's voice scratched a little.

Blake went to put Jaxi down, but his father stopped him.

"You're fine sitting right there. How's Marion? She okay?"

"Ma's fine, no new injuries. Although she's going to be upset when she hears they recast her arm, to be sure it was still set proper. She's got extra weeks to wait until the new cast comes off."

Mike's face said it all. "Hell, I should have been more careful."

"Don't go blaming yourself. Those moose are damn near invisible, right until they jump out and commit suicide," Blake commiserated. "It's not mating season so you couldn't have expected it, and that corner is a scary son of a bitch to take. We're all just glad you weren't killed. Maybe a busted leg and head aren't too high a price to pay."

"Leg? Marion break a leg too?"

Blake shook his head, worry creeping in. "You didn't notice you're wearing rather stiff long johns, Dad? It was a clean break but you're carrying plaster now too."

His dad shuffled the sheets to examine the thigh-to-foot white cast. "Well, hell. Nope, didn't notice a thing until now. Damn pounding in my head is drowning out everything else calling for attention."

"Yeah, well, you may have a concussion, but they said that should clear up plenty quick." Jaxi shifted in his arms, and Blake snuggled her in tighter, brushing back a curl that had fallen over her face.

He looked back at his dad to see a rather large grin waiting for him.

"So, does the fact you're finally holding that girl in your arms mean you're over being worried about what you never needed to worry about in the first place?" Mike leaned back, his smile stretching from ear to ear.

"You knew? You knew I wanted...?" Blake trailed off. Just how much did he want to talk about this with his dad?

Mike snorted. "Son, the entire county has known for years you had it bad for Jaxi. I don't know if it's because you're our firstborn or what, but you have a bad habit of trying to do what you think will please everyone else. You can't do that without missing out on what's going to please the people that are the most important to you."

He sat and thought that through for a minute. It was true. Small issues still poked him. "You don't think she's too young for me?"

"*Pfftt.* How much older am I than your mama?"

Blake frowned and couldn't come up with an instant answer. "I'm not sure, sir."

Mike nodded. "Right, because it doesn't matter one bit if there's a difference between us. Is the age thing what's been holding you back all this time? I wished I'd known. I didn't understand how you could be so stubborn to let her loose for so long. Heck, even your little brothers thought about—"

"I know what they were thinking and that's finished. Jaxi and I are..." Blake hesitated again, this time because he wasn't sure what to say. They were lovers, heck, they'd talked about babies.

But he didn't know where they were, right now.

Mike raised a brow. "You're what? Don't tell me you need a little more time to figure this one out. After all the girl's done the past few years to get ready to be the best rancher's wife possible?"

This conversation was too full of missing information for Blake. He felt as if he was the one with the head injury. "You want to explain?"

Mike pointed at Jaxi. "She took me for coffee the summer after her high school graduation and showed me a couple flyers from the local colleges. Asked me to mark the classes that would teach a woman to be a real help around a ranch. Someone able to pitch in, make sure things got done, and done right.

"She and Travis had just broken up, and I wondered if she was trying to get back on his good side or something, but when I suggested that, she laughed in my face. Well, politely—you know how she is. She said she'd been with Travis for one reason, and since they were through she was going to concentrate on something more important.

"Every semester she brought me another one of them flyers, and sometimes she'd mark a few classes to see what I thought—and some of them were plenty interesting. She's spent three years working and training for the position of rancher's wife. Hate to see all that training go to waste. Or get picked up by someone else smart enough to see what a treasure they've got waiting for them."

Blake kissed Jaxi's temple, and she cuddled in, sighing lightly. It seemed he was a bit more stupid than he'd dreamed. He needed to think this through a little more before committing to anything, but being with Jaxi felt awfully right.

Curiosity tickled for a minute, and he looked into his dad's happy face.

"So, what kind of classes were 'interesting'? I don't think those were the cooking or horse-care kind."

Mike shook his head. "Oh, no, you need to ask her. I was sworn to secrecy. You've got yourself a damn good woman, son, and I hope you don't do anything to mess it up."

Blake sat back more comfortably, the beating of Jaxi's heart solid against him as he and his dad discussed work plans for the next couple of weeks at the ranch.

The sound of a throat clearing jerked Matt to a stop. Discovering it was Daniel who sat in the dark of the living room was a whole lot better than being caught sneaking into the house at three a.m. by his ma or dad. No matter that he was twenty-eight, some things never changed.

"What you doing still up?" Matt whispered out of habit, since the rolling thunder of their dad's snoring wasn't shaking the rafters.

Daniel nodded toward the chair across from him, and Matt took a seat. "Waiting for you. Blake phoned about thirty minutes ago to confirm everything's okay. Ma and Dad had an accident."

"Shit. Bad?" Matt leaned forward. "Why didn't you call me earlier?"

"Didn't want to worry you until we heard more details, but they're fine. Blake says they're banged up and under observation for the night. The emergency crew thought the situation was worse at first than it turned out, so they got taken to Red Deer. Blake's driving back with Jaxi tonight—"

"Jaxi? She went along to check on Mom?"

Daniel smiled. "Sounds like more than that went down, but just so you know, we'll be starting work in the morning without Dad, and Blake if he's not up to the early rising."

Matt leaned back and stared out the picture window, the lights of the outbuildings faint in the darkness. "You still think about Sierra?"

His brother's light chuckle surprised him. "Well, that's a change in topic. You know what? I've been far too busy to worry about old girlfriends. Sometimes I wonder if she regrets calling us off, but then again..."

Matt waited. "What?"

"It's one of those things. She had stuff that was all-important to her, and I never knew. It's not like we didn't talk. We discussed all kinds of things. And yet out of the blue it was so important that any kids we had be hers? It made me wonder how much I really knew her. How honest we'd been up until then, or if we'd only been acting."

If this had been ten years ago, they both would have been razzing each other for talking like this. Matt's urge to tease vanished as doubt rocked him. "Just used to being with each other?"

Daniel rose to his feet and stretched. "Well, I'm not talking about something like you and Helen. Sierra and I only went out for a year, but yeah—I thought we'd covered all the bases. Truth was, she wanted something I couldn't give her, and I'm not talking about kids."

"That blows, by the way." Matt couldn't imagine. He didn't want kids anytime soon, but to know you didn't have the shot, not even down the road?

His brother shrugged. "It is what it is. I can't change the situation, so I have to deal. I'll spend my time on stuff I can affect. Hey—speaking of which. Ever since Dad loaned out the Peter's place from under us, I've been wondering. You planning on moving in with Helen anytime in the next while? We promised the house only up until Christmas, but I've been thinking that it would suck for a single mom to have to move her kids at that time of year. Dad could let her stay until the spring, but I didn't know how you felt about crashing in the basement that long."

Another hellish situation. "Daniel...I've asked Helen to move in with me a dozen times. Fuck, I've asked her if she wants to get married. She keeps putting me off, and while every time there's a logical reason, I just don't know what the hell is going on."

"She's still turning you down? Yeah. I can't help you there either. It's not like I have the best record with females. It's our younger brothers who still have the ladies falling all over them, and neither Travis nor the twins are looking to settle down anytime soon."

"Jaxi's got Blake on the run. Damn, that's funny to watch."

Daniel grinned. "He's skittish, but I think he'll figure it out eventually. They can work it out. She's got enough *oomph* to get him to realize what they both need."

Matt kept his mouth shut. Blake and Jaxi's issues were nothing like his and Helen's.

Daniel nudged him. "So what you think about staying here? You okay until the spring if that's what it takes?"

He nodded. That was a simple answer. "Hopefully I can convince Helen to move ahead sometime soon. But yeah, I'm okay with it. It's not like our folks are the type to stick their noses in where they don't belong. And if they're recovering from another accident, having us around while the twins are gone—I don't mind giving to the family. Ma and Dad have always been there for us."

Daniel thumped him on the shoulder and they headed downstairs.

Matt's mind spun with different scenarios. Moving in with Helen, taking on extra chores, watching Jaxi and Blake dance around each other. His family had always been a whirlwind of activity, but at the core—they *were* a family. He'd be there for them, just like he could always trust them to be for him.

He dropped onto his bed. Helen's hold out against getting hitched, first and foremost, was her family. Her parents' bad split, the way she felt her sister got treated better than her,
132

even before the divorce. He'd always thought she was being unreasonable to put off his proposals. That she should just accept the past and move on.

Maybe the weight of what she'd been through was more than she could easily put aside.

He knew his family could weather the tough times because they always had before—she too expected that the same thing that had happened before would happen again.

Betrayal. Hurt.

Matt lay back on his pillow to consider this new revelation. Still seemed to him that moving forward meant leaving the bad parts of the past behind, but if she hadn't made it to that point? Who was he to judge her for it?

Even this far-fetched idea of hers to try a ménage. She hadn't gone around him, hadn't simply cheated on him. It might be unconventional, but in her own way she'd shown she cared about him. Her request wasn't what he wanted, but he needed to accept it for what it was—a sign of respect.

It was far too late now, but come morning he would give her a call. Let her know he loved her, without using the word love, then do his damnedest to help her get over the past and head into the future with him.

Chapter Thirteen

Jaxi slipped a final peach half into the jar, topped it up with syrup and sealed the lid. Placing the jar with the others in the large pot on the stove, she closed the cover with a hum of satisfaction. She still had a couple of hours until supper, and after this last canner was done, she was caught up on her work.

She gave a little hop to sit on the counter, eating a ripe peach while she waited for the water to reach a boil before she could set the timer for the last batch. Juice dribbled down her fingers and chin, and she was slowly licking it off when she spotted Blake standing in the doorframe of the kitchen.

Watching her with hungry eyes.

Heat welled inside.

"You want a peach?" She held out a ripe fruit and beamed at him as he padded closer. He took the peach from her fingers, placed it carefully on the countertop and lifted her hand to his mouth, licking along the edges and between her knuckles. He opened her legs, pressing her thighs to the side as he slipped against her body.

"Just the sweet juice."

He lapped along her chin, short little strokes like butterfly flutters over her skin. Jaxi closed her eyes and enjoyed the sensation. It had been a long day with little sleep last night, between the loving and the worry of the trip to Red Deer.

Mike and Marion were stuck in the hospital for at least another couple of days. Blake had brought Jaxi home and set out the work schedule for the boys based on Mike's suggestions and their usual routine.

The last time she'd seen him that morning was when he'd kissed her goodbye after breakfast. A sweet, lingering kiss that had made her toes curl. Having the resistance between the two of them over, and finally being together, made satisfaction settle deep in her soul. They hadn't had a chance to finish their conversation—the one where she confessed she loved him and he hadn't said much back. It didn't seem the thing to poke him with while they'd hurried out the door to Red Deer, all worried about his folks. And she'd slept the entire trip home.

But somehow, from the way he'd been acting, she didn't think she needed to be too concerned.

"You didn't stop for dinner. Want me to warm something?"

Blake licked her neck and her collarbone. He unbuttoned her shirt. His fingers smoothed over her skin as he pushed the fabric aside to reveal her bra.

"I see what I'm looking for and it's plenty hot already." He slid the shirt off her shoulders to the countertop. "I like your bra, Slick, very lacy and pretty pink, but it's a little too nice for what I have in mind."

While he kissed, he brushed his fingers around her back, and the cool air of the kitchen flowed over her as he undid her bra. As if fascinated, he tugged off one shoulder strap at a time to let the cups fall away from her breasts.

"Blake?"

"I had something real interesting planned yesterday when we got interrupted." Blake lugged a tall stool from the corner of the room and returned to his spot in front of her. His head lined up with her breasts, and he hummed with satisfaction.

135

"We've had that stool since I was little. Ma used it to let us get a better reach on things, and it works as good now as ever. Maybe even better since the treats are sweeter."

He cupped a breast in each hand and lowered his head to cover the exposed surface of one with his hot mouth. Jaxi braced her arms behind her on the counter as an electric shock pulsed all the way to her womb. He alternated sides, lapping and sucking. She shut her eyes and enjoyed his intimate touch.

"Keep your eyes closed."

Blake slid away, and somewhere nearby a drawer opened and closed. She debated peeking when drops of liquid touched her skin, rolling down the swell of her breast. Moisture trailed to the tip of her nipple and clung there, cool in the moving air blowing in the window.

She opened her eyes to see he had the peach in slices. He'd crushed one piece between his fingers, letting the juice land on her body.

"Close your eyes," he warned.

Jaxi laughed before squeezing them shut. And waited.

Moist heat flicked as he lapped at the juice. Blake followed every sticky sweet line with his tongue, licked her skin clean, covered her with kisses. His fingers rolled her nipples, pinching and teasing. Ripples of desire spread through her body; her panties grew damp. The sound of something bumping and rattling slowly filtered though her sexual haze. The canner was ready, the water boiling.

"I've got to set the timer."

"How long you need?" he asked around a mouthful of breast.

"Thirty minutes."

He drew back with a satisfied suck. She looked down to see him stare at her with admiration, his hands still supporting her.

"Blake?"

"I'll tell you when thirty minutes are up." He stood, knocking the stool behind him to the floor. He plucked her off the counter and carried her to the dining room, laying her on the solid wood table. He opened the button on her shorts and tugged until they slipped off, leaving her clad only with the matching panties to the bra he'd discarded in the kitchen.

"Blake Coleman, I hope you've got your brothers working on something that's going to keep them far away from the house. Ohhh!"

He'd slid her down the table to where he usually sat, her panties suddenly dangling from his fingers.

"Nobody's going to show up here for a while. I want to see you, Jaxi. All of you. I want to sit at my place at the table and remember touching and sucking your pretty pussy. Everyone will wonder why I can't stop smiling." He shifted her slightly to get a better view.

"Open yourself for me."

Jaxi flushed. She already sat naked on the table where she'd shared Christmas dinners and birthday cakes with the Coleman family. She let her legs fall open and used one hand to slide her curls apart.

He leaned forward and licked, and her leg twitched so hard it slipped off the table. He smiled at her.

And did it again.

Sensations wrapped around Jaxi to meld into one enormous collage of emotion and touch. The pot bubbled on the stove, the canning jars rattling as they processed in the high heat. The windows were open, and a light breeze blew though the house, ruffling the curtains before coiling over her heated skin. Blake licked and sucked, slipped a finger inside her sheath and pulled her cream up and over her skin before rasping hard with his tongue. Time stood still as he loved her with his mouth, his fingers, his patient touch. She shook as her release came, waves of pleasure he drew out by licking again and again.

Then he stood, dropped his jeans, and slid in.

His cock was hot and hard, stretching her, as he forced his way into her body a little more with each stroke. She was attempting to meet him, trying to match with his timing, when he touched his fingers to her clit and rubbed.

Bursts of pleasure, sharp and fast, broke over her. He held her by one hip and leaned into the table, pressure mounting, his movements growing desperate, frantic even. He thrust hard enough the table rocked. He drove deeper still and shouted. His semen, hot and wet, bathed her inside as she shuddered around him again, her passage squeezing him tight.

Blake dropped his hands, one on either side of her body, and breathed hard, still buried in her body. His eyes caught hers, the grey storm clouds swirling. She gasped for air, her breasts jiggling with each breath she took. A trickle of moisture escaped from where they connected, and she tensed.

He'd done it again. They'd done it again. No protection.

He gave her cheek a gentle caress before he pulled out and tucked himself back into his jeans. Without a word he slipped her panties back on, helped with her shorts before carrying her back to the kitchen and assisting with her bra and shirt. Every time she tried to speak, he stroked a finger over her lips or brushed her to silence with a kiss.

Once she was fully clothed, he lifted the canning pot from the stove to the hot pads and helped her remove the steaming jars to the sideboard to cool with the rest of her labours.

He took her in his arms and kissed her senseless one final time before grabbing another peach from the countertop and strolling to the door.

"Supper at six thirty?"

Jaxi blinked in surprise, then nodded dumbly.

He took a big bite of the peach, then wiped the juice from his chin with the back of his hand as his eyes twinkled at her. "Peaches. My favourite."

He winked and scooted out the door, leaving Jaxi a little dizzy in his wake.

Chapter Fourteen

Blake jingled the contents of his pocket as he waited by the bay window in the sitting room. Jaxi had the table all ready for supper, the smell of chili and cornbread filling the air with spicy tones. The woman could cook all right.

More ways than one.

"Hey, Blake. Time to ring the bell?" Joel looked much better than the last time Blake saw him, eyeball deep in muck.

"Jaxi's not here yet. Let's wait until she's back."

Joel nodded and broke the crispy edge off a piece of corn bread. He looked Blake over while he nibbled on the tidbit. "So…?"

Blake stared back.

"You're not going to tell me how good it was, are you?"

"Shut up."

Joel snickered. "No, I figured as much. You're lucky she's wanted you all this time or I would have given you more of a fight after last night." He backed away as Blake took an involuntary step in his direction. "I'm teasing. I'm glad she's here and I'm glad she's with you. Jesse, on the other hand, was a tad more upset we went home alone last night."

"Alone? Yeah, right. That's why I saw the extra car in the driveway when Jaxi and I headed to Red Deer. Who'd you bring home? And please tell me there was more than one girl between the two of you."

"If you don't kiss and tell, I won't either." Joel winked before pulling a face. "Actually, Jesse did go home alone. He didn't seem to want to play anymore after we left you. Not even with the sweet thing we found on the dance floor who was very willing to join us both. I left the bar before he did."

"I don't want the details."

His little brother shrugged. "Whatever. Just didn't want you to think I've got any issues."

Blake shook his head slowly. There was one thing they needed to address. "Jaxi told me you'd agreed to play the game last night as a lesson for me. You pushed the limits there. A lot."

"Yeah, well, we never realized having you watch would make the fooling around that much more intense. Plus she was so damn responsive. Jesse did go a little further than we'd intended—the whole situation felt so good we kinda lost track." Joel looked at Blake and grinned from ear to ear. "She's yours and all, but, holy shit, last night was hot. I've never had a game of pool turn out like that before."

"Joel Coleman, I'm going to wash your mouth out with soap if I ever hear you mention last night to anyone again. You got me?" Jaxi swung into the room. Her long legs were bare to thigh high in another pretty sundress, this one bright red.

Joel leered at her for a minute, spun her in his arms and gave her a quick hug. "Yes, ma'am. I'll be good." His stomach grumbled loudly, and he dropped her to her feet again. "Permission to ring the bell?"

"Ring away, then help me get the drinks to the table."

She turned and settled in Blake's arms for a kiss, nuzzling close as a kitten. Blake drank in her scent. The concerns of the

141

past faded with each indication the walls he'd built between them were made of nothing but straw. Being wanted, being accepted so clearly—he wanted to soak in the sensation. Glory, and gloat even, in her bold-faced declarations.

It annoyed the hell out of him that one thought kept popping up and poking him in the nuts, ruining his buzz.

She'd dated Travis first.

All the Coleman boys had a similar cut. Solid features, clear lines. In their immediate clan, the twins were the fairest with their dark blond hair, but the other four were clearly family. And he and Travis, other than the age difference, looked a lot like twins themselves.

Blake couldn't bear to discover Jaxi had been chasing a dream all these years. Trying for a substitute for Travis.

She tugged his hand and he blinked. He'd been woolgathering while his brothers arrived at the table. He escorted Jaxi to her seat before joining the others and digging into the spicy food before him. An ear-to-ear grin stretched his face as he thought about the afternoon and Jaxi lying naked right about where his bowl now sat.

She was hotter than any five-alarm chili.

"You think Dad will be able to help at all this harvest or should we plan on finishing without him?" Matt asked.

"Let's plan on going it alone. He won't be driving machinery with that monster of a cast, although I imagine he'll be impossible to stop from helping completely."

Daniel scooped more salsa and chips onto his plate. "I'll finish the outstanding furniture order. It'll take most of tomorrow, but after that load is done I'll have time to help out wherever I'm needed in the fields. I think we should hold off on accepting more requests for the shop until we know for sure we're got things under control."

"Agreed."

Blake relaxed into his chair, his gaze on Jaxi as she sat across from him. She looked around constantly, checking the table and the food, eyeing the boys and the expressions on their faces. She caught him staring and blushed.

He chuckled softly. She'd sat naked on this table three hours ago. Now she was blushing while he looked at her fully clothed. She was too good to be true.

Talk continued for a bit before Blake turned from his conversation with Daniel to check again on Jaxi. The content expression she'd had at the start of the meal was nowhere to be seen. He followed her gaze. Both Travis and Jesse looked as if they'd swallowed a bug.

"Can I get someone to help dig beets tomorrow?" Her voice sounded falsely bright and Blake paused. What was going on?

He nodded toward Jesse. "He should be able to finish the fences by dinner. After that he can give you a hand."

Jesse ate slowly, all his focus on his plate. Jaxi laid a hand on his sleeve to get his attention and he jerked away. He shoved his chair back and rose. "I'm not real hungry. Got chores to finish in the barn."

Avoiding Jaxi's eyes, he stomped from the dining room.

The sound of forks on plates grew loud in the suddenly quiet room. Travis wiped his mouth, then threw the napkin on his plate. "Well, I may as well go too. Thanks for supper, Jaxi. Appears you still know how to cook up some heat, when you want."

She sucked in a quick gasp and Joel placed a hand on her arm.

Blake was on his feet in a flash. "Travis, what kind of rude-ass remark was that?"

His brother shrugged. "Didn't mean anything. I'll be in the barn if you need me."

His footsteps echoed across the floor, the door slamming shut behind him.

Matt shook his head and turned to Jaxi, whose face had gone white. "It's nothing but Travis being an asshole again. You know how he gets."

Jaxi nodded silently and poked at the food on her plate. Her big eyes looked suspiciously as if she was holding back tears.

"Excuse me." She slipped into the kitchen, her head down.

Blake made to follow her, but Joel held up a hand. "Let me. Please, Blake. I can at least ease her mind about Jesse. I know what he's thinking, and he really doesn't mean to be a shit."

Then there were the three of them. Blake glanced at Daniel and Matt, at the unfinished meal in front of them. Silently Daniel gathered plates together. Blake's stomach was tied tighter than he thought possible.

"I don't think I've ever had a meal at this table end like that."

Daniel snorted. "It ain't always been roses either, Blake. What did you expect? You won and they lost. Give them time."

He grabbed the load of dishes and headed for the kitchen.

Matt cleared his throat.

Blake turned to him. "You planning on offering me advice too?"

"Depends if you need it or not. I wanted to know. This thing with Jaxi, is this a keep-to-play or a play-to-keep thing?" Matt asked.

"Why is everyone expecting me to propose to the girl the day after we—"

144

"Don't be such a stupid shit. Because Jaxi's the kind of girl you should have proposed to before you took her, that's why." Matt's anger seemingly blazed out of nowhere as he rose to his feet. "You've had the woman dogging your heels for years. It's been clear to everyone she's head over heels in love with you, and more than willing to admit it. You're the bastard holding your relationship back, and I think you're an asshole if you don't get your butt in gear and face the truth. She may be hotter than the peppers in that chili, but she's a good girl. Treat her like one."

Matt stomped from the room, leaving Blake utterly alone.

He rose and paced to the window. The irony of the mess was he'd already had his own plans in place before all this unsolicited advice came his way. He jiggled the contents of his pocket again. It appeared he now had to deal with his brothers who were acting like idiots, as well as his own stupidity.

Outside, the sun painted the family land with bright colours, turning it into a picture before him, everything orderly and neat. His father and grandfather had worked hard to make the Coleman land a success. His brothers were right. This wasn't the first or last time the family would have to deal with having differences of opinions. Strong-willed, bullheaded bastards, all of them, with his name firmly on the top of the list. He headed to the barn to do some damage control.

With a short stop in the kitchen first to give Jaxi a kiss and a hug.

Travis sprawled on his butt on the straw-strewn floorboards, blood pouring freely from his nose. Jesse wiped at his mouth and glared at Blake, who'd just hauled his brothers apart. Jesse spun on his heel and headed for the door.

"Oh no, you don't." Blake yanked him to a stop by the back of his collar. "First you tell me what this is all about, and then we're going to settle any troubles you two have with me and Jaxi."

Travis and Jesse exchanged angry glances, but neither of them spoke. Travis heaved himself to his feet and tried to staunch the flow of blood. He backed away to stand warily as Blake eyed Jesse.

"Me and Travis had a difference of opinion. We're done." Jesse spat at the floor, his tongue licking at his bruised lips.

"Nothing else to say?" Blake demanded.

"Travis is the King of the Assholes. Happy?" Jesse snapped.

Blake barked out a laugh, "We already knew that. Of course, it looks like we need to put your name up for the title as well. You think you could work a little harder to hurt Jaxi? If you tried, you might beat Travis out of his crown."

"I don't have an issue with Jaxi," Jesse insisted.

"Well, it didn't seem that way to her."

Jesse bent his head against the wooden sidewall and stayed quiet for a minute. When he finally spoke it was toward the straw-covered ground at his feet.

"Blake, you need to back off on this one. I'm happy for you, I guess. But last night it could have been me making love to Jaxi. How would you have felt?" Jesse looked up at him, his blue eyes dark with emotion. "She's been a good friend for a long time and I'm not about to stop caring for her but...I got a taste of something I'm not gonna be able to forget overnight."

His whole body had gone rigid. Blake nodded slowly. He could sympathize with Jesse's hurt. He waited patiently, letting the words come as Jesse found the strength to let them free.

"I'm trying to do right by her and you. Give me time."

"I can do that."

Jesse's eyes flashed with one last burst of emotion. "But if you hurt her, you need to know I'll take you apart, then I'll take her away."

Blake hauled Jesse into a bear hug like he was a kid again and held on tight. They clung to each other, two grown men both needing the reassurance of family. It took a while before Jesse relaxed in his grip, his short, angry breaths of frustration slowing. Finally, he slapped Blake's shoulders and stepped away, head held high.

"I've never been so glad to head back to school as I am right now. It would kill me to watch the two of you spooning all over the house for the next couple months." Jesse wiped his fingers over his mouth again before examining them closely.

There was no way Blake's smile could look anything but forced. He was thrilled at having Jaxi in his life, but hurting his brother hadn't been his intention. "This will last a little longer than that."

Travis cackled, a harsh brittle sound. "Damn right it'll last longer, if she's got anything to say about it. Stupid, stubborn—"

Blake's blood rose to a boil. "You stop right now or I'll pick up where Jesse left off and pound you into the dirt. Whatever your problem is, you watch how you speak to Jaxi from here on. You got an issue, you tell me and we can take it outside. I'll knock the shit out of you anytime you like, but you leave her alone, you hear?"

The final thorn in his side stood across from him in the form of one younger brother with a shitty attitude and way too much history with Jaxi. Right now swinging a few fists sounded like a fine way to work off some steam. But when he'd seen her in the kitchen before coming outside, she'd made him promise not to bash anyone.

Damn woman already had him tied to a ball and chain.

"You got something more to say?" Blake asked. Quietly. Dangerously.

Travis kicked a seed sack. His eyes flashed. "You've been so damn righteous the past few years it's made me sick. Everyone knew Jaxi was setting her heart on you and yet you ignored her for some damn stupid reason, pretending she wasn't the one you wanted—"

"I thought she was still in love with you," Blake roared. "I thought she was trying to hook up with me because you'd broken up with her and I was the next best thing."

Travis's jaw dropped, his eyes black with anger. "You stupid son of a bitch."

Jesse moved between the two of them, wary and watching.

Travis shook his head and spat to the side. "You deserve every bit of pain you've experienced. Both of you. You know, if it didn't hurt so damn bad, that would be the funniest thing I'd heard in years. Jaxi pretending to be in love with you because she was still in love with me? Lord, listen to you. Damn." Travis wiped at his eyes, his voice shaking as he spoke. "She couldn't have done that, you ass, because the reason she went out with me in the first place was because she couldn't have you. Every time she kissed me, every time she touched me, she was closing her eyes and pretending she was with you."

"Stop. That's enough." Jaxi's voice cut through the chaos.

Three heads whipped in her direction. She'd changed into blue jeans and a T-shirt, and she looked sad and broken.

She stepped toward Travis and stared at him for a long time. "I'm sorry. That's not how it started. All the old-timers in town told me I was too young for Blake. That I should find someone closer to my age, so I tried. I thought that maybe if I was with you it would be enough. But it wasn't."

"*I* wasn't enough for you," Travis choked out.

Jaxi nodded slowly. "It was wrong, and I'm sorry I caused this wall to build between you and Blake. I should have known better. I should have just told you."

"You did tell me, remember?" Travis spat the words. "You called out his name while I was touching you."

Jaxi's head snapped up, and her whole demeanor changed, her quiet expression hardening. She marched forward three steps to face Travis, pulled back her fist and decked him on the chin. Travis reeled backward but kept his feet.

Her response was a bare whisper in the open air of the barn. "Don't you push me too far, Travis Coleman. You want to air dirty laundry in front of your brothers after all these years, then it's *all* going to come out. Every last sordid detail. Be careful, or your secret life won't be so secret anymore."

Blake shifted position, getting between his brother and his woman. He didn't know if he should assume control or let them work this through.

She continued talking to Travis, the tone of her voice all the more frightening by its softness. "You're such a self-centered bastard. You twist the truth so far you forget where it started, and you've begun to believe the lies you've told. Face it—I wasn't enough for you either."

Travis glanced up nervously. Blake's head pounded. Something was royally screwed here, beyond anything he'd imagined. "Jaxi? What the hell is going on?"

She tucked herself under his arm, burrowing her face into his chest for a moment before lifting her gaze to meet his. "It's okay. It's old business between Travis and me, and it's water under the bridge. No need for you to worry."

"Jaxi." Travis's voice shook as he spoke. "I didn't want to give you up. It wasn't you."

149

She turned in Blake's arms, keeping herself wrapped tight in him. Standing in the midst of the three brothers she had clearly chosen his protection, his comfort. Blake hugged her, his heart ready to burst. Travis had been a substitute for him, instead of the other way around. All this time he'd been worrying and picking at a wound that hadn't even existed. He drew her closer.

"Travis, let it go." Jaxi breathed out a long sigh. "We've both said enough, and it was never my intention to hurt you again. Let's just agree to let it go."

Jesse snickered from the corner where he leaned on the wall, watching the whole insane situation unfold. "Jaxi, you are one hell of a woman. You got three grown men tied up in knots 'cause we've all been head over heels for you at one time or another."

She threw him a dirty look. "You're not helping, Jesse."

"It's the truth."

"Yeah, well, the truth sucks." Travis plopped down on a bale.

"So, what do we do now?" Jaxi asked. "I can't stick around and force your family apart."

"What?" Protests rose from all the brothers.

Jaxi drew away from Blake slowly, shaking her head as she hugged her arms around her body. "Your family has been rock solid for years. There's no way I'm willing to come in and screw it up. It was never my intention to mess with anyone's life. I committed to help Marion, but I'll make sure I stay away from all of you. I can drive out early every morning and stay—"

"What the fuck are you talking about?" Jesse stepped forward, a scowl covering his face. "You're not going anywhere. Is she, Blake?"

She sure as hell wasn't, but turning into a caveman right now wasn't what she needed. The hurt in her eyes, the fear hovering around her, broke his heart and he wanted to wrap her up and protect her from any more chaos. Like a bird on the verge of taking flight, he caught her to him gently, cradling her against his torso. "You and me need to talk, Slick, but let's finish this off once and for all. Jesse, you got a problem with me and Jaxi being together?"

Jesse paused, his tightly coiled body poised before them, his hair and eyes wild. "You really want him, don't you, Jaxi?"

Her blonde head bobbed, and Jesse breathed long and hard before raising his gaze to meet Blake's. "No problems. You're a lucky man, and you'd better treat her right."

He blew a gentle kiss toward Jaxi, squared his shoulders and left the barn.

Travis still sprawled on the bale. Dark eyes flicked between Jaxi and Blake, and he answered grudgingly. "I've got no problems with it either. I'm sorry I was such a fool, both now and years ago." He stood and shuffled toward the door. "I'm not going to lie and say everything is wonderful and I'm happy for you and all that.shit. It hurts, burns like a brand inside me, but maybe a little time will help. I'm jealous as hell."

He stopped and chewed on his lip for minute before raising storm-filled eyes to meet Jaxi's. "Thanks for not saying anything. Someday...but not yet."

"I know, Travis. When you're ready." Angel-soft words, tender.

Travis strode away, leaving Blake alone with Jaxi as she shivered in his arms.

Chapter Fifteen

For long minutes Blake held Jaxi close, the familiar scent of the straw and the tack and the earth itself easing away the frustration and tension of the last hour. Whatever secret Jaxi and Travis shared, it was staying that way for now.

He wasn't sure he was upset about that either. It seemed there was a lot about Jaxi that was still a mystery. He hadn't realized how much she'd impacted Travis, how involved Jesse had become while Blake stubbornly pushed her away. His father had been the one to point out her training, and only recently had Blake noticed the way the community rallied around her and looked to her for help.

The bigger question was, did he really know the woman he had fallen in love with?

Blake knew he would work the Coleman ranch after his father. Had always known as the eldest son he had the privilege and responsibility to keep the family together and strong, leading them into the future. For the first time the picture looked a lot larger than just deciding what crops to plant in what fields and when to buy and sell stock. The family needed him to set the pace inside the home as well. Something his father had demonstrated by doing what was right even when it was tough.

A deep sense of remorse hit him. It appeared as if he'd fallen short on his calling in more ways than one.

He stroked his hands over Jaxi's hair, loving the way she fit against his body perfectly. Loving the smell and the feel and the rightness of her in his arms. There was nothing wrong with their bodies' reaction to each other, but that was another problem, another mistake he had made. He had let his body dictate his reactions since the beginning of this relationship with Jaxi. First in wanting her and refusing to deal with that truth properly, then giving in too quickly.

After approaching the whole situation wrong, now he would have to pay the price to make things right. He needed to step back so they could progress forward together properly.

Damn, he wanted her. But he wanted what was best for her even more.

Blake cupped her face in his hands and gently kissed her. Sweetly. When she would have crowded against him and offered more he resisted, holding himself back. It might kill him, but it needed to be done.

"Jaxi, we need a breather. I think what we've got happening between us is what we've both wanted for a long time, but we need to be sure." He led her to a bale, then sat across from her to watch her face. Watch the expressions that flitted there for him to see plain as day. The fear written all over her was strong enough to choke off his throat. "Hey. Don't look like that. I'm not letting you leave the family because you think you're tearing us apart. We had a misunderstanding as brothers. It's not the first time, and it's probably not the last. We'll get over it and move on."

Her misery twisted into a small smile. "You guys are good at fighting."

He nodded, dropping his volume. Trying to put what ached inside him into words. "And I'm not calling us off as a couple—just changing the pace. We're both guilty of moving too slow for many years, and now we've rushed like a Chinook blasting through the area."

She took in a quick breath, shaky with laughter. "Yeah, that kind of fits. But—Chinook winds blow through fast, and then they're gone."

"Oh, hell, I don't mean that at all. With all my heart I want this to be a forever thing between you and me."

Jaxi waited. He touched his knuckle to her cheek. "So...I'm going to court you. I'm going to woo you."

"But I'm already..." She raised a shoulder. "Seems as if you should already know how I feel about you. I told you straight out that I love you. Wooing seems like something you need to do with another woman, not me."

He clasped her hand in his. "You've spent years imagining me the way you wanted, while I was too scared to even be around you for fear of how I'd react. I don't agree you've had enough time to see the real me."

"I know what you're like, Blake, I know what kind of man you are." Jaxi insisted.

"Do you? We haven't done things together on a regular basis since you were about sixteen. Since I decided having you around me was dangerous."

A flicker of confusion passed over her face. "Dangerous?"

He lifted her hand to his lips, kissing her knuckles, his tongue stroking between her fingers. "Uh-huh, way too risky. You weren't ready for me and I wasn't ready for you."

He turned her palm over and pressed a kiss to the center before folding her fingers tight, closing his hand over hers.

"Go on."

"My idea isn't something you'll dislike, Jaxi. I'm talking about spending time together to play and work and just be. I want you to be sure this is real, that it's not something you've dreamed about for so many years you risk everything to see the dream come true."

She stared at him with those big eyes of hers, silence all around them. His stomach tightened. What if after everything, she decided she didn't want him? What if giving her time meant in the end he would lose her?

Even though the thought made his gut ache, he realized he loved her enough that he'd give her up. He would miss a piece of his heart forever but if she needed something other than him, he'd let her go.

In the meantime he was going to take his best shot at convincing her to say *yes*.

Jaxi wrinkled her nose. "So, what does this...*wooing*...look like to you? Are you going to call at my bedroom door with flowers and chocolates? Escort me to the movies so we can make out in the theater?" She cast her gaze down at their linked fingers. "Are we going to make love?"

Damn, she had to ask that question. His body knew what it wanted, but he didn't think that was what the answer should be.

"I'll bring you flowers and chocolates if that's what you want, only I'll bring them to the door of the guest cabin. You're going to move out of the house, and I'll move back in. You'll have more privacy there, and yet you'll be close enough Ma can call you if she needs you."

Jaxi protested and he laid a finger on her lips. "We can go to the movies, or we can go fishing. We can enjoy long rides and fix fences together, as long as I don't have to sit in the dirt after every fence post."

She snorted for a moment, her smile returning.

Blake stroked his hand over her cheek, smoothing her skin, tangling his fingers in her hair before he dropped his lips to hers again. The kiss was deep and needy, a joining together of hearts and souls. Not desperate and hard but desperate and soft. Lingering, caressing and more meaningful than any kiss Blake had ever given or received in his life.

They both drew back at the same time, breaths mingling as they remained inches apart. Blake reached deep for the strength to finish the job he'd begun. "I can't promise I won't touch you, but let's try to keep sex out of this. We don't have any troubles in the physical compatibility department. We need to see if we've got everything else it's going to take to last forever."

His thumb stroked her lips tenderly, sweetly. She kissed it and nodded acceptance with little jerks of her head.

Their foreheads rested together, and Blake breathed in her scent, storing the sensation of that moment for the days ahead.

A sudden realization struck him and he snorted. "So, Slick, in the kitchen you made me promise I wouldn't throw any punches tonight. You planning on explaining that right cross to Travis's jaw?"

The twinkle returned to Jaxi's eyes, and she shrugged mischievously, one brow rising high. "You never made *me* promise not to hit anyone, now did you, Blake Coleman?"

He stood and lifted her, swinging her in circles as their laugher rose to the heavens.

Chapter Sixteen

Wooing. What the hell did that mean when every time he looked at her his body lit up and his brain shut down?

Blake gave himself a mental smack. That's *exactly* why they were doing this. Because it was more than the sexual attraction between them that he wanted to play with.

He pulled to a stop in front of the fanciest restaurant in town and winked at Jaxi. "You stay right there."

She giggled. Honest to God giggled, and he fought his own amusement. Yeah, this had been plenty of fun—to take the time to build on their attraction and let themselves move one step further. Heading to a lonely bed each night when he wished he was curling up next to her was the rough part. But learning new things about Jaxi had been delightful and intriguing. He didn't want to just ask her what she'd been doing and learning over the past years, he wanted to find out as they went along.

They'd gone for walks. Sat on the banks of the creek and fished. And now, a week into the wooing, it was time for a little high-class experience.

He tugged open the truck door, and she slipped out before he could catch her. "You're supposed to let me help you down."

She lifted her chin, mischief all over her face. "Oops. Okay."

Before he could say another word, she was back in the cab, sitting forward and blinking expectantly at him. "Oh, my hero. What a big truck you have. I'm so *so* far up in the air."

"Stop that."

She grinned. "Would you assist me, dear sir? I'm afeared that it's too far a journey for my delicate little self."

Delicate little self—horse hockey. That from the woman who had helped muck out stalls for three hours the previous day in addition to her house chores? "You're looking for a spanking, miss."

"Yeah, but since you said that was out of the question for a while, I figure I'm safe."

Minx. He offered his hand, and she took it, spinning her legs toward him and delicately lowering herself to his side. He couldn't stop staring at the long length of skin showing. "You wore that miniskirt on purpose, admit it."

She blew him a kiss as she tucked in her shirt and smoothed the skirt. The twinkle in her eyes increased as she shimmied closer. The tight shirt emphasized every curve of her body, the deep scoop of the neckline showing off the perfect swells of her breasts.

He opened the restaurant door and led her into the dark elegance. All eyes turned their way, accompanied by some smiles, some frowns. The flurry of attention their direction hadn't died down yet. One of the joys of small-town living—any new match-up was an attention getter, and Blake had been single for long enough he figured the biddies would have a heyday for a good two to three months, not to mention that it was Jaxi he was squiring around.

They were seated in front of one of the fireplaces, Jaxi's chair to his right. They picked up their menus even though Blake knew exactly what he wanted. This wasn't his usual stop for a meal, but the few times he had come in he'd discovered the steaks they served were thick and juicy. His favourite, outside of barbecuing himself.

Jaxi wrinkled her nose. "You sure you want to eat here?"

She stared at the menu as if there was something disgusting on the page. Blake leaned to see if she had something different than him. "You don't see anything you like?"

"Well, I'm kinda distracted by the rather large numbers down the side of the page screaming at me."

"Oh no, don't you even look at that part." He snagged the menu from her. Damn, it was like taking his parents out. Skinflints, the lot of them. "If you're going to do that, you're ruining the whole idea of going out to a fancy place."

"But I can cook just about everything on that menu. And for a lot cheaper."

"You can, but then we can't visit and talk, and there'd be dishes to do afterward. This is supposed to be talkin' time, not complaining-about-the-cost time."

"But it doesn't make any sense—"

Blake leaned back and crossed his arms. Jaxi's chin lifted in the air as she cut off in mid-sentence.

"I want to take you out for a meal, and I don't want to hear another word about 'this costs so much' or 'I could cook that'. Then pick something you can't cook—that would work, right?"

Jaxi nodded slowly. "Do I get to pick for you too?"

Damn. There went the steak he'd been drooling over. The garlic mushrooms—he could almost smell them as they floated away. "Of course. Why don't you pick something you can't make, then for our next date I'll pick something we can cook up together—we'll set up a restaurant back at the ranch house. You good with that?"

Mischief streaked her face. "You sure about this?"

He hesitated. He'd never looked that close at the menu before, going straight to the steaks and eight-ounce burgers. "What kind of frou-frou stuff you planning on tormenting me with?"

Jaxi straightened her face and held out a hand for the menu. "Oh, I think I can come up with something we can both enjoy, if you're willing to be a little flexible."

Blake stared at her as she opened the folder and her gaze raced over the page. Every now and then she smiled, or frowned, and he fought to keep from twitching.

"I don't think I can listen to this." Blake stood as the waiter approached. "You order, I'm going to wring out my kidneys."

Jaxi licked her lips and waved him away. "Take your time. I changed my mind. This is going to be fun."

Fun. Yeah, like the time they'd been castrating and the snippers slipped and nearly took off more than he'd intended.

He took his time, then wandered back slowly, wondering if he should nab a menu to peek over and figure out exactly what she was going to torture him with.

"Psst. Blake."

Off in the corner he spotted a set of frantically waving hands. Two of his brothers stuck their heads from a hidden booth. Joel grinned like a maniac. Travis wore a more sarcastic leer.

"What the heck you two doing?"

They exchanged sheepish gazes. "Chaperoning."

Blake scratched the bridge of his nose with his middle finger and listened with amusement to their whispered squabbling about whose bright idea it had been in the first place. "Seems more like stalking than anything. I doubt we need much watching, but if your wallets want a kick in the teeth—be my guest."

Joel groaned. "You bastard. Had to pick the most expensive spot in town...and Jaxi can cook most of this for way cheaper."

Bloody hell. "I've already heard that argument." Blake stared at Travis. His bruises, courtesy of Jesse, had faded to purple and green. "I'm surprised to see you here."

"Matt had some kind of urgent date pop up and cancelled at the last minute. I had nothing else happening tonight and Joel wanted company. I have no objection to eating steak while I watch you make an ass of yourself." His anger was still there, simmering underneath the surface. Travis jerked and swore at Joel before deliberately changing his expression. Breathing slower, relaxing his shoulders. He grimaced, then glared across the table. "Sorry, Blake. Momentary lapse. Joel, keep your fucking feet to yourself."

"You said you'd behave. Be thankful I'm not wearing shit-kickers."

"Ass."

"Takes one to know one."

Oh, Jesus. Blake couldn't believe this. It was as if they were all still in their teens at times. "Well, this has been wonderful, but I'm kind of busy right now."

"You going to take her dancing later?" Joel leaned forward and stared down the length of the restaurant. Blake followed his gaze to find candlelight reflecting off Jaxi's face. His heart thumped hard a time or two, just thinking how lucky he was to even have this chance. After all the times he'd pushed her away.

"Why? You boys want to show us how to two-step? Who's gonna lead?"

Travis snickered. "Can't be Joel. He lets Jesse do all the leading from what I hear."

"Oh, that's a load of bullshit, right there."

The squabbling started again and Blake gave up. He had better things to do with his time than referee his brothers. "Have a nice night, boys."

He ignored their continued whispered suggestions as he made his way back to his table. Jaxi had changed her seat and was now in the chair across from him. "You didn't like the view?"

"Didn't want to sit next to you. I thought it would be more fun to have a clear shot of your face as the food arrives."

Oh sweet mercy. Heaven save him from this disaster of a *get to know Jaxi better* idea. "That's a marvelous idea."

She reclined in her chair and crossed her legs. One high-heeled shoe dangled from her toes as her foot bounced lightly. He stared in admiration, considering whatever it was that she'd ordered as a minor penalty to pay for the view he was enjoying.

At least, he thought that until the waiter arrived and placed a single plate between them. The pristine white surface had a tiny mound of twisted tube-like brown lumps in the middle. A thin line of dark sauce had been artistically drizzled over the entire thing in a zigzag pattern.

Jaxi leaned forward to examine the offering more closely at the same time he did. "What's that?" he asked.

"Not telling."

Blake grimaced. "Now, that doesn't seem very fair..."

Jaxi shook her head. "If you know ahead of time what it is, you might be prejudiced to not like it just on principle."

She picked up her fork, speared a small portion and placed it in her mouth. She chewed slowly, staring at the ceiling, not giving any indication if she liked it...whatever *it* was...or not.

Damn weird foods. Blake poked himself one and popped the piece in his mouth.

Fire licked over his tongue and shot from his nostrils. The sauce was a twist on a savoury barbecue, but the actual lump was like chomping on strands of combustible fiber. His throat burned as he swallowed, and once his water glass was empty he reached without thinking to drain Jaxi's as well.

She stared, eyes widening. "What's wrong?"

Once his throat was no longer an inferno, he lowered the glass with a sigh. "Nothing. Just enjoying our appetizer."

Her mouth twitched, and she took another piece, lifting her fork in the air in salute before closing her lips around it. She licked the utensil clean and watched him closely.

Blake shuddered and valiantly took another try. There was no way he would admit defeat with Jaxi happily chewing not even two feet away from him. What kind of wimp was he anyway?

This time the chunk wasn't anywhere near what he'd gotten the first time out. Tender and only a tiny bit spicy, the meat fell apart in his mouth.

"Hey, that's not bad." He prodded the food with his fork, leaning in to take a closer look.

"Blake!" Jaxi slapped the back of his hand. "Stop poking at it and eat."

"But—" She gave him a stern look and that was all the warning he needed. He straightened up right quick, still trying to figure out if there was a way to tell the demon chunks from the angelic ones without sacrificing what was left of his tonsils.

Every bite after that was an exercise in anticipation totally different than he was used to around Jaxi. Her fire burned him all the time. These bastard hunks of meat seemed to have no rhyme or reason.

"Just so you know, I only ordered one thing for each course. I figured we could share." Jaxi blinked innocently at him.

He laughed. "You minx. That's an interesting way to get around the prices."

"I have no idea what you mean." She sipped her wine, batting her lashes, a sly smile sneaking out. "The appetizer was ginger beef, by the way."

The empty plate was removed and a new dish brought. He barely heard her, the new item of potential torture holding him in awe. "Is that...still alive?"

She covered her mouth with a hand, her eyes shining like diamonds. "Oh dear."

"Well, not that I'm saying no to trying whatever it is that you've got arranged here, but you got to understand that usually I kill the beast before I toss it in the pot."

Jaxi shook with her laughter, tears running down her face. She wiped at her eyes with her napkin, before taking a deep breath and grinning widely. "Thank you for taking me out, even if this kind of fancy-schmancy thing isn't what I'd want to do all the time. It's been a lot more fun than I thought it would be."

Blake tried to ignore the simmering pot that sat in the middle of their table, concentrating on her face instead. Nope. Didn't work. The steam rising between them created a haze that kept drawing his gaze downward. He lifted his spoon and bravely scooped a bit. "You're welcome. Gonna be nice this time and tell me what this is?"

Jaxi hesitated, before nodding agreement. "Stewed monkey brains."

"Ahhhh…" He jerked to a stop with the spoon barely touching his lips. Five seconds later and he would have spewed all over the pristine white tablecloth. Her choked laughter started again, and he shook his head, delight filling him.

Damn woman. Damn *fine* woman.

Only two more courses to go. Heaven help him.

Chapter Seventeen

Matt clicked on the light beside the bed. The tiny loft apartment over the back barn hadn't been used for a long time. He'd gone out earlier in the day to make sure it was clean and ready.

And to wonder just how fucked he was in the head to have agreed to arranging a ménage.

The lighting in the room was low, and Matt stared at Helen, wondering if the flush staining her cheeks was fear or anticipation. "You okay?"

She hesitated. "Yeah. It's just...strange. Thinking about being with someone other than you."

"I know." The idea of sharing her still sat funny. Matt pulled her close, nuzzling against her neck. "We don't have to do this, you know. Gabe ain't gonna say a word if he shows up and we tell him to take a hike."

He didn't want to admit how much he really wanted her to choose that option. To tell him that this was all a mistake and she was madly in love with him and him alone.

Damn it, he wanted the words *and* the actions.

Helen linked her fingers around his neck and pulled him in for a long lingering kiss. He nibbled on her lips, taking the time to lick and caress. Stroking with his tongue, teasing with his fingers across her lower back. Tiny brushes on the bare skin between the bottom of her T-shirt and the top of her low-rider jeans.

He kissed his way along her jaw, sucking the dangling lobe of her ear into his mouth. "You want to be naked before he gets here?"

She shook her head. "No. I think...I want to go slow."

Matt scooped her up and carried her to the bed. Before Gabe arrived, and after he left, Helen was going to be all his, even if he had to share her for a short while.

He laid her down, crawled beside her and stared into her eyes. "I've wanted to be with you since we were little tykes riding the school bus. You'd hop on at the second-to-last stop, and I'd try to make it look like a real coincidence that there was an empty seat next to me. Didn't let you know that I'd just kicked Daniel out of the way to make room for you."

She laughed and cupped his face in her hands. "Matt Coleman, why does every session of lovemaking seem to include a trip down memory lane?"

Because she'd been there his whole life. He grinned. "I like travelogs."

Matt rolled over top of her and settled between her legs, their hips separated by their clothing, but the heat more than enough to be felt between them. He rocked slowly, the ridge of his cock riding the seam of her jeans, and she opened her thighs and closed her eyes.

"Yeah. I feel that so good. Oh, Matt, it's like you know everywhere to touch, everywhere to make me squirm."

He did. All her hot-buttons were so familiar to him, what she liked, what she wanted. Except for her request for this ménage—that one had come out of the blue. "You okay me getting you off quick the first time?"

She smiled, bright blue eyes flashing. "Now what kind of silly question is that? As if I'm going to turn down a patented Coleman orgasm."

They laughed together, then paused as he caught her gaze. He wanted her to know how he felt, even if she didn't want to hear the words. She was going to know in spite of him not saying it.

He tugged her T-shirt aside, unsnapping the button of her pants and slowly undoing her zipper to allow him to slip his hand under the waistline. He stayed overtop of her undies, cupping her heat as he took her lips again. She flicked the tip of her tongue against his, tiny motions that he matched with increased pressure, his middle finger bearing down on her clit.

She gasped. "Oh yes, that's the spot. More."

He forced the wet silk between her folds, molding the fabric to her, teasing with a light touch that maintained constant pressure. Helen writhed on the bed, her head twisting slowly from side to side as he kept up the pace. Then he leaned over and covered one breast with his mouth, biting her nipple through the fabric, and she came, shaking under him.

When she opened her eyes, it was to sigh with satisfaction, one hand cupping his cheek.

He was leaning forward to kiss her again when the knock sounded.

Something went icy cold inside, until she flicked a glance toward the door. Her breathing sped up, a flush rose over her neck. The intensity of her arousal answered the unspoken question of whether she really wanted this or not.

Matt kissed her, hard, intense, before scrambling off the bed and heading for the door. He cracked it open just in time to spot Gabe shift position, straightening up from where he'd reclined against the railing of the landing.

Gabe rubbed his mouth. "Am I invited in, or no?"

For one long second Matt stood motionless, tempted beyond belief to tell his cousin to take off.

Helen pressed against his back, her hands wrapping around his waist. Her lips, warm and gentle, made contact with his neck as she kissed him. She wanted this, and he'd give it to her. This once, and only this once.

He motioned with his head and pulled the door open. "Party for three, ready to begin."

Gabe slipped past, clutching his cowboy hat in his hands. Helen remained tucked against Matt's side, and he pulled her around to face him.

"Anything makes you uncomfortable, you want to stop, you tell us. Any time, any time at all, alright?" He stared into Helen's blue eyes, searching for signs of fear.

She licked her lips and nodded. "I trust you." Helen glanced over his shoulder at Gabe. "And you're..."

He waggled his brows. "Lucky?"

Matt laughed at the optimistic tone in his cousin's voice. "Bloody lucky."

"That wasn't the word I was looking for, but if you like it, okay." Helen leaned against Matt and threaded her fingers through his hair, tugging until his mouth came down to her level.

Matt took a deep breath and concentrated on giving his lover the fantasy she'd asked for. He kissed her, and she trembled as he caressed his hands up her waist, over the sides of her breasts. He swallowed her groan of delight, bracing himself as she pressed closer. When he realized she'd shifted position because Gabe had stepped behind her, trapping her between their two male bodies, a streak of desire hit Matt hard enough to make his knees shake.

Okay, he'd wondered how he would feel, having another guy touch Helen. But right now, he was amazed at the intensity of the excitement sweeping him.

Matt stepped back, leaving Helen leaning against Gabe's chest. Her eyes were wide, mouth open in an O. She shivered, her head leaning to the side as Gabe kissed her neck. There were goose bumps on her arms, and small gasps of pleasure escaped her lips, her eyes closing as Matt observed for a moment.

"I'd love to say hello properly and get a taste of your lips." Gabe gazed over her shoulder at Matt. He nodded agreement even as Helen answered.

"If you're going to ask permission every time before you do anything, this will be a very slow evening."

Gabe turned her to face him, winking lightly. "Oh, there're times to go slow and times to go fast, and I'm pretty sure Matt and me can show you which is which. Don't you worry, darling."

He leaned in and kissed her, a bare brush of his lips over hers. Gabe pulled away and Helen leaned after him, as if trying to make the contact last longer.

"Ah-ah. You ain't in charge here. Kiss Matt and show him how much you appreciate him setting this up, and then we'll see about what's coming next."

Helen twirled away from Gabe, her mocking pout fading as she stepped to Matt's side and pressed herself against him tight. She cupped his face and smiled sweetly. "I do think you're pretty damn special, Matt Coleman. Thank you." She kissed him like she was on fire, tongue and lips taking him by storm. Matt curled an arm around her and let her cling like a burr as they shared a moment—hot and wild. No holds barred. Gabe could have been a million miles away and all that remained was need and heat. When they drew apart, Matt gasped for air.

Gabe brought Helen back to his side and took her lips again. This time, his kiss was as heated as what she'd just shared with Matt. Gabe caught her hands and pulled them down by her sides, and Matt got inspired. He tugged off his belt and clasped her wrists himself, looping the leather over and over until she was bound, helpless to free her arms.

"Nice trick, Matt. You two use ropes often?" Gabe unsnapped the top button of Helen's blouse, his gaze fixed on her face.

"I like ropes. Matt's good with them."

Gabe smiled. "All cowboys are good with ropes, darling."

"Some more than others." Matt ran a finger down her back. "And this ain't about ropes, is it? It's about trying something brand new."

Helen laughed. "Then why'd you tie me up?"

Matt kissed the side of her neck gently as he grabbed on to the sides of her blouse. "Because I wanted to."

He jerked the material apart, buttons flying, skittering over the floor. One more move brought the fabric off her shoulders to bunch together at her wrists.

"Oh, yes. That's a very pretty sight." Gabe hummed approvingly as he stroked the top swells of her breasts, fingering the edge of the black bra Helen wore. When he leaned forward to lick the path his finger had followed, Helen shivered.

Gabe pushed aside one shoulder strap until the bra cup fell away. Helen arched her back and pressed her chest forward, the exposed nipple tight and peaked already.

"Sweet, sweet darling." Gabe licked the tip lightly, then surrounded her and sucked.

Helen whimpered and tugged at her restraints.

Matt pulled the other side of her bra off, giving Gabe a full view of her tits. Gabe took up the challenge and cupped her, lifting one side and then the other to his mouth. The material from her blouse and bra hung around her waist, bunched up and awkward. Matt pushed past the fabric to slip his hand into her pants again, the moisture from her previous orgasm and her current arousal making her soaking wet.

He skimmed a finger through her folds. "You're enjoying this, aren't you?"

Her reply turned into a gasp as he thrust in two fingers, heel of his hand hard to the apex of her mound. Matt stilled, listening to her panting breath as Gabe suckled and bit lightly, her nipples gone dark with excitement.

Matt tugged her pants awkwardly with one hand, only to find Gabe taking over the task. His cousin unzipped and slid her pants from her hips, stripping her bare from the waist down. He stopped to stare in admiration. "Oh, darling, you are full of surprises, ain't you?"

Helen widened her stance, leaning heavily on Matt, exposing herself to Gabe's intimate inspection. "You never seen a woman who waxed before?"

"Oh, I've seen it. Just didn't expect to find your pussy all bare and delicious. Matt, I'll say it again, you are one lucky man."

Matt pulled his fingers out to circle the tender skin of her labia before thrusting in again. Gabe leaned closer and licked, and Helen shuddered. It took the two of them only minutes to have her trembling, body shaking as her sex squeezed around his fingers, a cry of satisfaction escaping her lips.

Matt stripped his belt away from her wrists, then tugged her shirt and bra free.

Gabe was already stroking her curves, her skin shining velvety smooth in the low lighting. "God, I need some more of you."

Helen crowded against Gabe's body as he kissed her again. Matt stepped away until his back hit the wall, watching. Weighing his reaction. That was his lover, his woman, being caressed by another. Gabe's hands stayed gentle on her torso as he lowered his hands to cup her ass and squeeze the rounded cheeks.

Anger struck for a second, and Matt beat it down. Helen dropped her head back and the moan of passion whispering from her lips firmed his resolve. She wanted this—he had to be strong enough to make this everything she wanted.

Because goddamn if he'd ever, *ever* do it again.

In spite of his jealousy, his dick was rock hard. Matt felt no discomfort undressing in front of his cousin—as if Gabe gave a shit. Hell, they'd found their first *Penthouse* together and shared the damn thing, jacking off without a care not even two feet from each other. Matt tore down his jeans and kicked his feet free, stripping away his briefs and moving back to reclaim Helen.

She turned to face him, chest heaving, eyes wide. She smiled, a wicked, dirty expression that was quickly explained as she dropped to her knees before him.

Shitfuckdamn. Matt stared down as she wrapped a hand around his cock and pumped, her eyes never straying from his. "You planning on doing something with that, sweetheart?"

She licked her lips. Stroked again, cupping her other hand under his balls and rolling them. Without answering, she moved. Her lips circled the head of his cock, and she slipped forward, engulfing his entire length at one go. Hot, wet pleasure slid up his spine, and his vision blurred. She sucked hard, clutching his ass, nails digging into his skin. Behind her, Gabe was busy ridding himself of his clothes.

Matt threaded his fingers through her hair and held on tight, pulling the strands back to get a cleaner shot of his dick disappearing into her hot mouth. "Suck me. That's it. Good and wet. Get my balls now—hell yeah, that's the way."

He thrust a little deeper. Helen tilted her head back to allow him to bump the back of her throat. Stars floated before his eyes, and pressure built in his balls. Another thrust, and another. Helen arched her back and let him fuck her mouth. He slowed. Took a long plunge deep into her mouth and held himself there with her nose tight to his belly. Her throat convulsed around him.

"Goddamn, that's the hottest thing I've ever seen," Gabe muttered.

Matt tilted Helen's face toward him as his cock pulled from her lips with a *pop.*

She panted for breath, but her gaze kept darting between him and Gabe.

Matt smoothed his fingers through her hair, the heavy weight of anticipation in his dick easing off. Taking a breather was a good thing—he didn't want to explode yet.

"You want to try him on for size?"

Helen nodded, not a word spoken, but anticipation in her eyes.

Matt stepped back, still holding her head, and Gabe replaced him, cock in hand. "You sure have a pretty mouth, darling. Show me how good you are."

He pressed the wet tip against her and she opened eagerly. Matt moved behind her, staying in contact, lifting her chin with a finger as Gabe slipped between her lips and groaned loudly.

Helen seemed eager to try everything, not simply rush to the final act. But even watching this—watching her give to Gabe—made it impossible to not want to dash forward. To hurry to the point they could shake his cousin out the door and be alone together.

He left their erotic tableau for a moment to strip back the bed sheets, tossing the pillows back onto the bed.

"Gabe—bring her here."

His cousin eased away slowly, pausing just before the crest of his cock emerged to press all the way in one final time. Helen moaned, clutching his thighs for balance as he pulled free.

Gabe lifted Helen to her feet and guided her to the bed, his still-erect cock pressed to her hip. Matt took Helen by the hand and yanked her against his body. He ignored Gabe, catching her by the back of the head and kissing her hard. Her erect nipples poked his chest as she scratched her way up his back, nails digging in.

He stared into her eyes as he slipped a hand down her torso to cup her mound. His fingers rubbed against the slickness there, and she undulated her hips forward, looking for more than his teasing light touch.

As one they tumbled to the sheets. Their limbs tangled as he kissed and caressed, moving them together until she shook with desire. That's when he rolled her belly down on top of the pillows, hips raised high in the air. He got her ready, his fingers skimming the crack between her cheeks. Pressed in the lube, slicking her up good, and his condom-covered cock as well. By the time it was his shaft pressing into her ass, Helen called out his name and came, just from his thorough preparation.

Satisfaction rolled over him as he clung to his control, the tight squeezes around him enough to make him go off like a firecracker if he wasn't careful.

Matt wrapped a hand under her belly and lifted, rolling them both until he sat on the bed and she rested in his lap.

"Oh my God." She dropped her head back on his shoulder, her thighs spread wide, feet dangling on the outside of his legs. "So full. Feels so good."

"You gonna feel even fuller." Gabe stepped forward, smiling that devil-may-care grin of his that twisted off the girls' panties. He was wrestling on a condom.

Matt gasped as Helen tightened around him again. "Jesus, Gabe, get a fucking move on, or this will be a chain-reaction performance."

He knew the moment Gabe touched her. She tensed, then relaxed, a gasp of pleasure slipping from her lips.

"Oh. My. *God.*" Helen lifted her hands to Gabe's shoulders, her fingernails digging into his muscles, red marks and white appearing instantly along the indents.

"You have the most amazing pussy, darling. Hold on for the ride. You ready?"

Helen nodded. Matt wished he could say the same. He was beyond caring about anything but the noises escaping her lips. The sheer pleasure as Gabe and he alternated their way in and out of her body. Tighter than usual, even slick with lube and the moisture dripping from her core. Helen grunted as their rhythm changed and they both fucked her, thrusting simultaneously. Pushing her over the edge and letting themselves go along for the ride. It was crazy and wild and over the top.

Unfuckingbelieveable.

At the end of it, Gabe pulled away to collapse onto the bed near the edge of the mattress, allowing him and Helen the majority of the room. In the brainless, sated moments that followed, he and Gabe dealt with their condoms, then returned to touch and caress Helen. All three of them lay flat out and exhausted.

"Thank you, darling."

That was all Gabe said as he planted a kiss on Helen's sweaty forehead. He didn't hit the bathroom, just pulled on his clothes and hightailed it out the door with a final wink and grin for Matt.

In the cleanup that followed, Matt worked patiently. He took his time to not only wash away all signs of Gabe, but to try and write himself alone into her heart. She snuggled in close, her lips tucked against his chin. The puffs of warmth from her mouth as her breathing slowed stroked him like perfumed air.

"Thank you, Matt."

He kissed the tip of her nose. "Was it what you'd hoped for?"

Helen was quiet for a minute. "Yeah. I guess."

She snuggled up again and was snoring softly in a few minutes.

Matt laid wake, too many thoughts in his brain to rest for a long, long time.

Chapter Eighteen

Jaxi crawled up on the concrete ledge outside the movie theater to wait next to Blake, resting a hand on his shoulder. "And I want licorice and the biggest damn bag of popcorn they've got."

She held her grin even as Blake gave her the evil eye. "You want more to eat after what you already put away back at the house? I swear you ate half a side of beef all by your lonesome."

As if. "Working around the ranch works up an appetite. Male or female. You should know that, oh Mr. Two ten-ounce steaks, three baked potatoes with all the works and... Now, how many pieces of pie did you eat?"

Blake twisted to stand between her legs. With the height of the ledge, that put their eyes at the exact same level, and he leaned forward to rest his forehead against hers. "Okay, fine. I won't tease you about being able to out-eat me if you promise not to count slices of dessert anymore."

Jaxi wrapped her arms around his neck and squeezed tight. Man-oh-living, this wooing thing or dating or whatever the heck they were doing had turned out to be a damn good time. It was everything she'd wanted.

He turned to greet Matt and Helen, keeping hold of her fingers in his. Showing off that they were together.

That was the most startling part of this whole situation. He'd been so resolutely staying away from her, she'd had no idea how much they could actually do as a couple. From chores to trips to town. The extra work it took to care for Marion's work hadn't stopped her from spending more time with Blake than she'd thought possible. And he seemed determined to not allow anyone to either ruin their dating or push them forward too fast.

Not even her. Which also sucked since she really missed having him touch her. She'd barely gotten to enjoy having sex before it had been taken from her. Masturbating when the oh-so-desirable man she wanted was nearby was not nearly as much fun.

"Glad you guys made it on time." Blake wrapped an arm around Jaxi's back and leaned on her legs. Jaxi smiled at Matt and made sure she held her expression firmly in place as she nodded at Helen.

"So, is it girls' choice or boys' tonight?" Helen gave Matt a gentle shove, her streaked hair fluttering in front of her face. "Because I'm not sure I'm up for some of the flicks playing here."

Oh God. Jaxi resisted the temptation to suggest the most violent and gory movie available. Something about Helen just rubbed her the wrong way. She resisted the devil on her shoulder for Matt's sake. "Well, I haven't seen any of them so I'm game for whatever."

Blake nodded his agreement.

Helen turned to examine the posters and Matt frowned at Jaxi. "What's wrong?" he mouthed.

Oops. Jaxi wiped her lips and shook her head at his questioning glance. She'd better work on her stage face. Her instinctive dislike for Matt's girlfriend wasn't going away, and every now and then her aversion showed.

She tugged Blake close, and he willingly leaned his ear toward her. "I'm going to the end of the line for a minute. I just spotted someone I need to talk to. You make plans without me, okay? I'm good with any of the shows."

Blake nodded. He lifted her off the ledge and gently lowered her. She savoured the sensation of rubbing against him briefly, longing for more.

She ducked past Matt and Helen. Halfway down the line she checked over her shoulder. Yup, as she suspected, Blake still had his eyes glued to her ass. She wiggled her hips hard for a second, and his gaze snapped upward, his mouth crinkling up at the corners.

Oh yeah. He was trying hard to keep them on target, but the physical attraction simmered all the time, just under the surface, and she saw absolutely nothing wrong with that.

"Hey, girl, what you doing?"

Jaxi pumped knuckles with an old schoolmate. "Well, he's about six foot four and..."

Eve laughed. "I heard you finally hit the jackpot. Good for you. Any tips on how to land one of the other Six Pack boys?"

She shook her head. "Now, you. I thought you'd decided the twins were nothing but trouble, and you didn't have the patience for Daniel to notice you were alive, and Travis is too much of a ladies' man. And you can't have Blake, so try one of the other Colemans. Moonshine Steve is looking hot these days."

They laughed and compared stories for a few minutes. Who was seeing who, which couples had split up. It was like going back in time, but Jaxi felt every minute of the growing up she'd done over the past years.

"Hey, I needed to find out if you'll be around for the picnic in a couple weeks' time. There's still a few spots open for helpers."

Eve nodded. "I've started university, but I'm back in town most weekends. Let me know where you need me and I'm there."

Jaxi gave her a quick hug before working the line, walking slowly back to where Blake waited. Her plan worked wonders—by the time she'd returned to him she had a dozen more names for the volunteer crew.

Blake had a dark expression in his eyes as he took her hand and pulled her close. She looked up in confusion at the change in his attitude. When there was break in the conversation with Matt and Helen, she tugged him to the side and pulled his head down to whisper in his ear. "Something wrong?"

His hands on her hips squeezed for a second before spilling around her to caress her back. He sighed, then lifted her chin. "I'm glad you're you."

Jaxi paused. "That's cryptic."

"Just don't leave me alone with Matt and Helen again, okay? I swear you could give that woman a bag of gold and she'd complain about how heavy it was."

Jaxi laughed against his neck. So she wasn't the only one Helen rubbed the wrong way. "I'll be like glue."

"You done all your visiting? Planning on sitting next to me for the show?"

"Of course." She poked him in the ribs, and his face lit up as he focused in and kissed her, right there in the middle of the waiting line. She wrapped her arms around him and gave back completely. It was like no one else was around—just her and him, and caring, affectionate touching.

"The doors are opening." Matt's laughter broke in and pulled them apart.

Blake held his hand toward her. Jaxi slipped her fingers into his and let him lead her into the theater. She smiled sweetly at the older couple she recognized who stood beside them as the two lines merged.

"Evening. How's your grandson doing with his therapy?"

Mrs. Bridges gave a quick nod. "Better all the time. Thanks for asking. Oh, and can you tell Marion I'll be by in a few days with that pattern she was wanting?"

"Sure thing." Jaxi waved and let Blake pull her along without even looking where he was taking her.

"You know everyone in town or just about everyone?" They'd stopped in front of the concession. Jaxi's stomach growled and his eyes widened. "Damn it, I thought you were kidding about still being hungry."

Warmth and contentment filled her. They chatted, teasing and joking easily. Waiting for their snacks, glancing around and pointing out *coming soon* movies they were looking forward to. By the time Jaxi had a full armload of food, she'd just about figured out what was out of the ordinary.

While he made her thrill with every touch and every glance, the heat tonight was something altogether new. It was...familiar and tender and less about wanting to roll around naked with the man and more about getting to plan for the future.

It felt different.

She had thought things through, but until this moment, it had never registered as a reality. How being in love with him meant all the different parts of being in love. Being by his side, not just now, but years from now.

The Bridges slipped into seats a few rows ahead of them, Mr. Bridges helping his wife in first. Careful, tender.

Jaxi blew out a slow breath and swallowed hard. She was going to be in tears if she wasn't careful. Somehow she had to haul in her foolish emotions before she ended up blubbering like a damn idiot.

Blake managed to balance his tray and still touch her shoulder to guide her to where Matt and Helen had saved seats.

She sneakily managed to avoid having to sit next to Helen. It made her sad that she didn't like the woman more, but she wasn't going to waste time figuring out why. She wasn't the one kissing the chick, Matt was, and if he was happy, that was all that counted, she supposed.

They were all seated, and she leaned into the protective circle of Blake's arm along the back of her chair.

"Blake. What are we watching?"

He chuckled. "Well, blood and guts were shot down by Helen, Matt refused the chick flick, and if I want to watch a historic anything I'll stick with the History Channel. You got action. That okay?"

That was more than okay. The last thing she needed tonight was a tearjerker. Action, tension. Those would be perfect.

Guns. Hmm, some guns would be good.

Chatter died around them, the lights dimmed and Jaxi caught a glance of Blake's profile lit by the flickering motions on the screen. His square jaw, the strength in his features. She stared, mesmerized. She thought she'd memorized his face long ago. Stolen glances at the dinner table while she was dating Travis. Times around town as he loitered for a few minutes, chatting with the men, and she'd stopped in some hidden space to watch him.

There was something new in his features she'd never seen before. The strength, still there. The almost frightening beauty, rough but undeniably attractiveness.

He turned to face her, and her breath caught in her throat. Something deep and dark rolled out from him and softened as she watched. He wasn't trying to be the man of the family or the person in charge. Hunger and need and a light filled with the promise of laughter right behind it shone in his eyes.

She couldn't inhale. It was too much, too powerful and beautiful. The corner of his mouth twisted upward, and suddenly it was all she could do not to throw her arms around him and never let him go.

He stole the popcorn container from her and placed it on the floor, then slipped his hand around the back of her neck and slowly, oh so slowly, drew her lips toward his.

"Hey. Down in front."

Jaxi cursed silently as Blake paused, their mouths less than an inch away from each other. Was that...?

"Oh, stop your whining. There's nothing happening yet." Jesse's light tenor tickled in her ears.

Joel snorted in response. "On the screen or in front of us?"

Oh lordy, this was not real. Jaxi swallowed hard for minute. Blake never lost his smile. "You want to pretend they just ain't there?"

He tugged a little closer and their lips met. Jaxi opened eagerly. Who the hell cared if they gave the twins a show? Served them right for coming out and crashing the party.

"If they keep that up, it's gonna be tough to enjoy the special effects."

Jaxi froze. Blake jerked back in a rush, and both of them spun to examine the row behind them.

"Now, Mike, hush. The movie's not started. It's just the trailers." Marion waved at them from two seats down, Mike grinning broadly at her side, his arm tucked around her shoulders.

He shrugged tolerantly. "Okay, fine. You kids go ahead and enjoy yourselves."

Jaxi turned to face the movie screen, placing herself as exactly in the middle of her seat as she could. At her side, Blake did the same, although he snuck his hand over to grasp hers. The upcoming movie trailers played across the screen, and she wondered when the time warp back to ninth grade had taken place.

His elbow bumped hers, and she glanced over, wondering what was going on. Then a complaint rose from behind them, and she grew even more curious. Blake squeezed her fingers, then guided her hand toward his lap.

She resisted. *Oh my God, no.* She'd been longing to touch him, but not in the dark of the theater with his entire family seated around them. That would be like some nightmare of a sexual experience.

He tugged harder and unless she wanted to make a huge fuss, she had no chance of winning an arm wrestle with him. She faced forward resolutely in the hope nothing would show up on the screen that would brighten the room enough to allow people around them to see her touching...popcorn?

His grin shone white against the darkness for a second before he turned and seemed to ignore her. But his fingers reached over hers and pulled some of the corn from under her grasp. Then he leaned back, and as she watched, a fast glint of something flew through the air.

"Fuck." Jesse gasped a second later. "Sorry, Ma. I meant, damn, something hit me."

His whispered complaint was all she needed to understand the rest of the story. Blake's shoulder was all warm at her side, his fingers held hers tight, except when they both took turns surreptitiously tossing popcorn over their shoulders, attempting to hit Jesse and Joel most often.

It was silly and childish, and one of the most right moments Jaxi had ever experienced in her life. No rules, no expectations. Just fun, and being literally surrounded by family.

She rested her head on Blake's shoulder and contentedly munched on another licorice stick.

Chapter Nineteen

Jaxi pushed through the laundry room door and jerked to a stop. Travis straightened up from the washbasin and turned to face her, his expression tight.

Oh my God. She hadn't just seen what she thought, had she? "What the heck—?"

"Don't. Just...don't go there." He grabbed a bloody shirt from the ground and tried to duck past her, but even with the basket in her hands she was fast enough to get in his path and block his rapid retreat from the small room. "It's nothing. I didn't think anyone was around, okay?"

She shoved the basket of clothes onto the top of the dryer and reached for him, batting away his hands as he tried to stop her. "No one was. I came in early to get a few things cleaned up while the house was still empty. Where the heck you been? Your dad was livid this morning when you didn't show up for chores."

As she spoke she turned him, tugging on his belt until his strong back was in clear view. A shudder shook her as she took in the damage. "Oh, Travis."

His shoulders sagged, all his bluster escaping like air from a balloon. "I don't want to talk about it."

"Of course you don't. When did you ever want to talk about these things?" She pushed him to the side and snatched up a clean rag, soaking it under warm water. "Fine. I won't ask questions, but I am fixing you up. Get over here."

The misery in his eyes was hidden as he bent forward to rest his elbows on the washer, giving her easy access to the multiple rows of welts crossing his back. The skin was swollen, broken in spots. Dried blood clung to him, fresh red oozing from where the barely set scabs broke away from the cuts.

Jaxi bit her lip to stop from blurting out all she wanted to say. Instead, she worked steadily, as gentle as possible as she pressed the cloth again and again to his flesh, softening and cleaning away the blood. A shiver raced over his skin, a low grunt of pain as she touched a particularly bad section where the cuts lay in crisscross fashion over each other.

She couldn't take it anymore. "Belt?"

He hissed as she used the cream from the first aid kit on the topmost line, careful to make sure she coated the welts thoroughly. "Thought you weren't gonna ask questions?"

"Yeah, well, I thought you weren't such an idiot to let someone mark you and then leave you in bad shape. There's supposed to be two sides to—"

"This is definitely talking you're doing. I know what it's supposed to be like, okay. It just doesn't always work the way we want it to."

Jaxi left her hand on his back, the warmth of her palm pressed cautiously against his skin in the hopes her touch would blunt the words. "You seem to have that happen a lot, Travis. Not work out the way you want."

He tensed, straightening up and twisting to face her. A pulse beat in the vein in his temple. "Sometimes it's been good. But yeah...my luck's been shitty at times. Someday that will change."

She stared at him for a moment. Whatever sexual attraction they'd had between them had been fleeting—on her part mostly because of his likeness to Blake. She still didn't know if he'd really cared about her or if having her around had been the ultimate cover-up to help keep his secret indulgences hidden.

Travis's dark eyes held hers for a moment before he dropped his gaze. "Thanks for your help."

She nodded. Moving was the only way to deal with her frustration. She pulled a clean T-shirt for him from the dryer, placing it on the metal surface. "Is there anything else I can do?"

Jaxi swallowed hard as he reached out a hand and cupped her cheek. He rubbed his thumb over her cheekbone, a light, delicate touch. It was less seductive than needy, as if he was attempting to draw strength from their connection.

He shook his head, but she felt it. Felt his plea as clearly as if he'd spoken.

"Oh, Travis." She pulled him against her and carefully hugged him. Just let the warmth of her body comfort him. She wasn't looking to provide anything more than compassion, but if nothing else he needed a human touch right now.

They stood, locked together. Travis's torso remained tense, but he dropped his forehead to her shoulder. She stroked a hand over his head, giving him the only thing she could—caring the only way possible. As if she were comforting a grieving child. Her heart hurt for his sake.

He drew a big breath and squeezed her one final time before opening his arms and stepping back. His eyes glistened with moisture, and she wiped at her own for a moment.

"You going to be okay?"

His response was somewhere between a laugh and a cry. "I always land on my feet in the end. Don't worry about me."

Jaxi caught his hand in his. "That's not possible. You can't just turn off worry."

His confusion was clear. "I thought you didn't want me? I thought you and Blake were together now?"

Jesus. "Don't be a stupid ass, Travis. I don't want you as a partner, but I do care about you as a friend. And Blake is—"

"Right here, wondering what the hell is wrong with you."

Jaxi spun toward the door. Blake leaned against the frame, his arms crossed in front of him. Travis cursed, soft and low, and quickly dragged the clean T-shirt over his head, keeping his back hidden from Blake's view. Jaxi winced on his behalf as the fabric hit his skin.

"Nothing happened. Jaxi was just helping me...clean a cut."

Blake scowled. "And if I was asking about Jaxi and you, right here and now, that would be a suitable response. But I trust Jaxi too much to even have a moment's thought that she'd be doing something wrong. I meant what the fuck is wrong with you in general? You didn't show this morning for chores, and the few things you are responsible for around the ranch you keep messing up. Damn it, Travis, it's time you grew up and took things more seriously. You're not a baby who should have to be told everything that has to be done."

He stepped into the room. Travis twisted away, the two of them traveling in opposition like predators circling each other. Travis stopped an arm's length from the door. Jaxi moved into Blake's path, and he wrapped an arm around her shoulders and tucked her against his side.

"I don't have to report to you where and what I'm doing." Travis's chin lifted, his words and attitude a million miles away from the broken boy she'd been comforting a few minutes ago.

"While Dad's out of full commission, yes, you damn well do report to me. We work together as a team, and you're not putting in the energy. Face that reality and whip your ass into shape. It's not only the family you're letting down, it's yourself."

Jaxi debated speaking up, but what could she add? Travis had screwed up. Whatever personal issues he was struggling with didn't mean he could mess with the rest of them.

Travis rolled his eyes. "Oh, yes, sir. I promise to get right on that. The growing-up shit. You have no bloody idea—"

"You're right. Maybe I don't." Blake's volume dropped to almost a whisper. He slowed and held a hand toward Travis. "I have no idea because for a lot of years you've been one of the 'little boys' back at the house with Ma and Dad, and I just didn't take the time to find out more. I have no idea what is going on in your life. I'm sorry for that. But I can't be expected to know more than you tell me. Until you let me in, until you and I find some common ground other than our blood and the fact we both work this patch of land, I'm not going to understand you."

Jaxi's throat tightened.

Travis was frozen in place by the door, his face rigid. "So that makes it all fine? That you don't know?"

Blake shook his head. "It makes it wrong on my side. And I'm serious about wanting to get to know you better, at whatever speed you're comfortable with. But I'm also serious about you taking responsibility for your actions around the ranch. You don't have to let me into your life this instant, you don't have to share all your secrets, but don't let us down on the job. If you need help, then ask."

Travis stared over their shoulders at the back wall of the laundry room for a moment, his fingers crushing the ruined shirt he'd grabbed. When his gaze returned, he glanced first at

Jaxi—a silent request for secrecy in the depths of his eyes. Then he nodded at Blake.

"I'll get my shit together. Sorry I blew off work today. It won't happen again."

Then he was gone. Nothing more about the family, nothing about his own personal hell. Jaxi turned her face into Blake's chest and held on to her tears by a thread. God, she ached.

He stroked her back and soothed her, lips brushing her cheek as he dusted kisses there. Light and gentle, a caress of comfort.

"I don't know why I feel like crying so hard right now." Jaxi forced the words out past her closed throat.

Blake's chest moved under her as he sighed. "I know how you feel. Realizing I've been a shit to him for years makes me want to weep as well."

Jaxi leaned back with a jerk. "What? You've been a good—"

"Good brother? Actually, no. I've been thinking about it since we had that argument in the barn. There're a lot of years between me and Travis and the twins, and it's been too easy since I moved out to concentrate on my life and only fit theirs in when it was convenient. The twins I've kept in touch with a little bit, but Travis? He kind of slipped under the radar, not just with me, but I think with the rest of the family as well."

Blake pressed his lips to her forehead. Jaxi thought he might be right. Even to her, Travis was a mystery in some ways. It had been three years since they'd really spent much time together, and other than him constantly having a new woman on his arm every few weeks—yeah, all she'd seen as well was the surface persona he wanted to show.

"So, what we going to do?"

He lifted her onto the washer so their eyes were level. "We're going to do the laundry."

"What?" Jaxi frowned. "I meant about Travis."

Blake squeezed her hand, then stooped to open the dryer. "It's in his hands now. I'll make sure I keep a little more aware of my brothers, but other than that, I can't make him tell me anything, now can I? So let's just move forward and hope that he chooses to do his job and at some point open up more."

He pulled clean laundry into a basket, squatting on the floor to reach the back of the machine. Jaxi watched for a moment as she rearranged some of her expectations and worries.

Then she hopped down and hugged him right there where he was, squeezing his neck tightly.

"Now, what's this all about?" he asked.

She kissed his cheek, then stood to deal with the basket she'd brought in with her. "You're a good man, Blake. Don't let anyone tell you differently. Not even yourself."

They stared at each other for a moment before turning back to the ordinary, everyday task of laundry. The pain in her heart didn't go away, but somehow, that was just fine. She'd trust Blake. Trust that Travis would choose at some point to come back to the family.

Chapter Twenty

Matt stared across the coffee-shop table at Helen. "You're headed where?"

"Edmonton. Just until next weekend."

He bit back his frustration. "You said you would help out at the picnic this afternoon. Going to be kinda hard to help when you're four hours away."

She picked at the rim of her paper cup, refusing to meet his eyes. "Well, gosh, what a shame. A community picnic. Be still my heart—I'll miss the social event of the decade."

"Don't be like that." Matt glanced at the tables around them to see if anyone had heard her snide comments.

"Don't be what? Honest? For God's sake, Matt, I don't want to spend all Sunday afternoon wandering out in the sun with the smell of horses and sheep and shit. I said I wanted to spend the day with you. I didn't think that meant I had to go country for the entire day. Again. So when the opportunity came up…"

Matt leaned back and stared out the window as he drank his coffee. His mind raced. He'd thought things had gotten better between them after the ménage, and for a few days, it seemed they had. Helen had been the most content he'd seen her in a long time.

But then she'd started making comments about how maybe they should think about moving. Only she wasn't talking about moving in together like he'd suggested, but moving away. Getting jobs in Calgary or Edmonton.

What was a rancher supposed to do for work in the city?

He turned his gaze back to look her over carefully. All the things about her that had attracted him in the first place seemed to be changing, and he wasn't sure quite what to do with this new Helen.

Even in the bedroom she was different, more demanding. Which was okay every once in a while, but being commanded to tie her up seemed to lose some of the spontaneity. He wanted to be involved in what they were doing, not simply servicing her requests.

But ordering her around was a lost cause. He didn't want to be one of those asshole boyfriends who assumed he could control her entire life.

"How you getting there?" Since it seemed she was determined to go.

"Darrel Aften is driving out. I'm hitching a ride with him. He's going to his cousin's. Dora and I go way back."

Matt swallowed the words wanting to burst out. Yeah, those two went way back. Dora was one of their high school classmates who'd been on a bus out of Rocky before the ink was dry on their diplomas.

Helen leaned forward, all excited to tell him about the things she planned on doing while away. Matt listened with only half an ear. Keeping a smile on his face took more effort than he thought possible.

Fine. She'd go away. When she got back they were going to have a serious discussion about the future, because this relationship wasn't growing the way he wanted. He wasn't

195

giving up on them, but for two people who'd spent so many years and so much time together, the paths they were walking seemed to be veering part.

It would be a fucking shame if he couldn't pull them back together.

The children led her through the maze, a dark bandana covering her eyes. The little fingers tugging her along were sticky from the picnic dinner, giggles rising as they guided her around obstacles toward the finish line. Suddenly there was an extra loud burst of laughter, and Jaxi smiled in amusement.

The past weeks had been better than anything she'd ever expected. Her work around the house had flown while at every possible opportunity Blake found time to romance her. Not only dinner, but dancing and horseback riding. Long walks in the fields where he'd teased to try and find out more about her schooling over the past years. She'd told him a bit, but there were a few things she thought better shown than told. She'd even suggested a game of pool at one point just to see his reaction...

"You ain't going anywhere near the pool hall for a good long time, Slick. My heart can't handle any more games right now."

Jaxi opened her eyes wide. "But you promised we could—"

He'd covered her mouth with a finger, followed by his lips, kissing her into oblivion.

And that's about all they'd done in the physical department. Held hands, snuggled on the couch watching movies. Kissed. It was a step backward, taking it sweet instead of sexy. She missed his touch, his intimate caresses, but she had to admit there was something intoxicating in seeing his eyes clouded with lust when she turned from washing dishes or doing chores and have him simply give her a gentle kiss. She knew no matter what clothes she wore, he found her attractive.

That he wanted her, but wanted to be *with* her more, shook her to the core.

A tug on her hand brought her back to the present and the picnic.

"Miss Jaxi? You gotta hold this now, okay? We'll lead you with the rope."

She smiled at the sweet sound of the child's voice. "Are we almost through the maze? I need to serve coffee and dessert soon, you remember."

The chorus around her all assured her she was nearly at the end, so she grabbed the section of rope they pressed into her palm.

More giggles and a few *shhh* noises rose before another tug led her forward. She inched ahead with careful steps, trusting the little ones to do their best, but knowing they might miss a gopher hole underfoot.

The sound of voices faded and she hesitated. "Are we still going the right way? Kids, what are you up to?"

The rope jerked again and Jaxi held back, wondering what had changed.

"Don't you trust me?" Blake's deep voice was unexpected and she sucked in air.

"Blake?"

His fingers linked through hers and a hand caressed her cheek. "Well, you've been playing with everyone else, I figured it was my turn. Follow me, not much farther."

Her heart thumped a steady beat at the easy tone in his voice. The tension she'd noticed building in him over the past years had faded away, leaving behind the man she remembered.

The caring individual with a wicked sense of humor and the patience of a saint. He must have been sexually frustrated. They hadn't made love since his *wooing* started, but he seemed content. She reached for him and clasped his elbow, tucking in closer to his side. His arm wrapped around her, and she blindly walked at his side with confidence.

She'd go anywhere he wanted to lead her.

"Blake, can I tell you something?" Suddenly it was important she share what she felt, what a joy it had been to find he'd been right about slowing down. Even though she physically ached for him, seeing him with new eyes had been the right thing.

"In a minute. Let me get that blindfold off first." He reached behind her head to untie the knot and his lips caressed hers, brushing back and forth tenderly. She opened her mouth a crack and slipped out her tongue a tiny bit, meeting his touch, tasting his flavor. They stood wrapped together kissing tenderly, slowly, savouring each other until he pulled back and she sighed in contentment.

"You need to open your eyes."

She looked around with delight. He'd arranged a blanket on the grassy bank of the river, a basket with food open to the side.

"I watched you. You were so busy helping everyone else, as usual, you never got anything to eat." He led her to the blanket and sat, patting the spot next to him.

"I'm supposed to serve—"

"You're supposed to be with me. I arranged it all in advance. Cari and Leo agreed to serve desserts. Jesse and Joel are working coffee, and the rest of the boys are doing cleanup." He held out his hand. "You, on the other hand, I have assigned a different task. It ain't going to be an easy one for you, Slick, I can tell you that now."

She joined her hand with his and snuggled in close, feeling guilty that she wasn't helping at the picnic yet ecstatic to be alone with Blake. "What's my task?" she asked.

He reached over her to grab something from the basket, the heat from his body covering her, and she couldn't stop from wiggling upward, letting their bodies touch. A groan broke from his lips as he sat back, desire clouding his eyes.

She gazed into the depths of his soul.

Blake breathed heavy for a minute, his chest heaving, his hands shaking as he handed her the sandwich. "I can see this task ain't going to be easy for me neither. Holy hell, woman, you're driving me insane." He collapsed back on the blanket, covering his eyes with one arm.

Jaxi nibbled silently. The blood pounding through her body made the sound of the river fade until all she heard was the constant thump of her heartbeat and the echoing throb in her core.

"I need to tell you something." He rolled on his side to stare at her. "I'm not sorry about teasing you until you caved, and I'm not sorry we made love, but I'm also not sorry you took over and made these past weeks special."

He chuckled. "That's the strangest 'not apology' I've ever heard. I'm not sorry either. About any of it."

She handed him a can of pop from the basket. "I need to ask you something. You said we needed time to see the truth about each other, to see if what we felt was real or just an image." His throat moved as he drank and Jaxi found herself having to swallow hard.

He made every inch of her tingle just sitting next to him.

"I did." He lifted a hand to play with her ponytail.

She closed her eyes briefly to gather her thoughts. Facing him square on, she held his hands tightly in hers. "Blake, what I've seen is a man I trust. A man who has the respect of both the community and his family. Jesse went off to school a couple weeks ago after hugging you to pieces and giving me a chaste peck on the cheek. He's got no bitterness brewing with either of us and I'm so grateful. That's because of you, because of the way you talked to him and shared with him. The way you treated me when he was around to prove you were the best one for me.

"Even Travis—God, the way you opened yourself up to him? I had no idea, but somehow you figured out what he needed. You haven't urged me to share his secrets, and you trusted me right when it was most important. You haven't asked me to give up reaching out to the others. You've supported me around the house and in the community. Heck, even today, stealing me away and making me relax. That's what you want me to do that's supposed to be so tough, right?"

He grinned at her with his new cocky smile that made her heart melt and her panties wet all at the same time. "Well, you do seem to have a problem with the word no. Using it with others, that is. Did you notice I had to find seven people to replace you?"

She lifted his hand to her mouth and kissed his knuckles. "What I've also seen is a man who put his sexual desires on hold, even when tempted by a very naughty tease. Your strength of character and your..."

She couldn't go on. Her throat was closing, and it all came down to one thing.

"I love you, Blake Coleman. I always have, but I know it more now than ever before."

Blake brushed his thumb over her mouth and she kissed it. He moved in close and nestled her alongside him, the hard length of his muscular body heating her up. She relaxed back on the blanket and stared up as his strong features broke into a smile that reached his eyes.

"I've got a whole lot to say about you too, but I'll start at the end. I love you." He leaned down and kissed her again, this time harder, his tongue dipping into her mouth and stroking hers. His hand cradled her neck, directing the angle to mesh them closer, nibbling and tasting each other until they drew back breathless.

Blake grinned at her and continued. "You're not a little girl, you're all woman. Not just your body but your mind and your heart. The only person I've ever seen work as hard as you is my ma, but she's nowhere near as good looking." He winked and she swatted him teasingly. "It's not just the energy you use when you serve others, but the way you pour in love. Everything you touch is better because you've been involved. It's humbling to see how much you love others and realize you love me too."

He kissed her nose, kissed her cheek, touched a finger to the moisture escaping from the corner of her eye.

"I could go on and on about how you care for my family so tenderly it makes me ache inside in the part of me that needs family to be number one. I can't just love you, Jaxi, I've got to love my family. I've got so much more to learn there about how to really be there for them, but the way you fit in and belong with us all is incredible. So important."

Her heart was full to overflowing. She closed her eyes to stop the tears from escaping.

His voice scratched. "Thank you for being stubborn enough to force me to see you belong with me." He lifted her to a sitting position across from him and clasped her hands again. She stared into his eyes, and he took a deep breath.

"Jaxi, I want to—"

A series of giggles broke the intimacy of the moment, and Jaxi snorted in disbelief.

"Miss Jaxi? You gonna come hand out the awards for the colouring contest?" A trio of children traipsed over the ridge to surround Blake and Jaxi. One of them crawled into her lap, another into his. The oldest of the three glared at Blake in disapproval.

"You've been kissing her, haven'cha?" he complained.

Blake nodded slowly and solemnly. "I have."

"Ughhhh. Doncha know girls got cooties?" he whispered in Blake's direction.

"Children, come back. I'm so sorry, I didn't know they were looking for you until a minute ago." Cari tried to round up the strays and shoo them away, even as she checked the details of the setting with interest.

Blake laughed out loud as the tyke in his lap wrapped her arms around his neck and clung to him. "Well, it's fine, Cari. I forgot Miss Jaxi was supposed to hand out awards. I guess we need to go and do that right now."

He rose to his feet and shifted the little girl to his hip, reaching a hand to Jaxi. Guilt at ruining his wonderful surprise rushed her, and she tried to make it better. "We don't have to go, Blake."

A chorus of disappointed cries rose from the children, and his playfully stern headshake brought more tears to her eyes.

"Of course we have to go. This is important, handing out prizes. Come on, kids, show me where we need to take Miss Jaxi." He nodded at Cari, and she winked before moving to pick up the blanket and basket. He lowered his voice conspiratorially to the little boy waiting. "You see, I haven't been in a colouring contest for a long time, and I can't remember where they hold it."

Jaxi ambled slowly, a child in her arms. Beside her Blake listened to the running monologue of the little waif, nodding and *aha*ing at appropriate times.

If this was what a family felt like...

Bring it on.

Chapter Twenty-One

Blake looked around the table with mixed emotions. Jesse and Joel had came home for a weekend visit. Ma and Dad were missing, out at the hospital for a check-up and X-rays for the afternoon. They had friends staying with them to drive them home in the evening. With their folks gone, Travis's absence was expected, but there wasn't much he could do at this point other than wait for his brother to come around. Blake turned to talk to Daniel about a new furniture order, the quiet conversation peaceful in the room. A soft touch brushed his groin, and he flicked a hand at it, thinking one of the cats had gotten into the house.

Jaxi's foot rested in his lap.

He jerked up quick, checked to see if Daniel had noticed anything, then snuck his chair in a bit tighter before he looked her way.

She talked quietly to Jesse, not a single indication anything naughty was happening. Certainly not something like her bare foot rubbing back and forth over his crotch until it was damn near impossible to concentrate on the conversation he was , pretending to hold with Daniel.

A hand waved in front of his face, and Daniel snickered. "You need more sleep. Jaxi asked if you wanted dessert."

He turned a hot glare on her that made her gasp.

"I'd love some dessert. I'll help serve."

He shoved back from the table and marched around to haul her from her chair. He didn't care it was clear he sported a hard-on he could hang a horseshoe from. She'd started the game.

He was going to finish it.

"You need any more help there?" Jesse called as Blake shouldered through the door to the kitchen with Jaxi hanging from his arms.

All the boys laughed and Matt complained, "I bet we don't get any dessert until it's gone cold."

Cold would be good right about now, because Blake was headed for spontaneous combustion. Having kept his hands off her for this long, he was ready to break. He dropped her by the sink and looked her up and down slowly, his gaze taking in the long length of her legs, all the way from her bare feet to the hem of her sundress.

"What's for dessert?" He circled her slowly, a finger trailing over her waist, over her hips. Up her back and along the bare skin exposed on the edge of the neckline.

Jaxi swallowed and dropped her head to the side. His hand rose to support her neck. Blake wrapped himself around her until she had nowhere to go but hard against him.

"Jaxi? You've got a bad habit of not answering questions."

"I was distracted..."

Blake kissed the beating pulse in her neck. "What's for dessert, and did you know that's a very sexy dress?"

Jaxi smiled. A mischievous expression that told him she'd remembered their first conversation about sexy dresses. "Apple pie and ice cream, and if you're asking if I'm wearing panties, you've got to find a setting a little more private than the kitchen."

"What's the matter? You never been naked in front of a crowd before?" he joked, smoothing his hands over her ass. No panty lines, but she might be wearing a thong.

Since the picnic he'd been scheming and plotting to get her alone and been frustrated at every turn. He'd almost given in to temptation and snuck into the guest cabin with her, but that wasn't how he wanted to finish this. Before long, he wanted to take them to the next stage.

It was time to move on. Oh hell, it was past time.

Jaxi slipped from his arms and served slices of pie onto plates. She had a little smile at the corner of her mouth, and Blake stopped even as he reached for the ice cream scoop.

She couldn't have.

"You never answered my question. You ever been naked in front of a crowd before?"

She stole the scoop from under his unmoving hand and added servings of ice cream to the plates, her smile turning into more of a smirk by the minute. He tugged the scoop out of her hands, picked her up and set her on the counter.

Eye to eye he looked at her. Leered, to tell the truth.

"Tell me."

"I took a modeling class to learn how to dress nice in something other than jeans all the time. I got asked to pose and there was—"

"You posed? For a Sears magazine or a—?"

Jaxi pressed her finger to his lips. "I posed for a group of artists. Nude." She grinned at him. "It was a really lucky circumstance because I wanted to take a dance class and one of the artists turned out to be an exotic dancer. I went to her studio and she gave me private lessons."

Blake was growing hotter by the minute, the ice cream in danger of melting to puddles from simply being in the same room. Holy shit, she knew how to exotic dance?

Did his dad know about this? Is that what he'd meant by "interesting" classes?

Blake pulled her off the counter and handed her a couple of plates of pie. She had no idea what she'd just let loose. The tentative plan running through his mind was okay, but this beat anything he could have devised, even with weeks of setup.

"Go deliver these. Then gather whatever you need to put on a show for me. I'll wait in the barn."

"The barn?"

"That a problem?" Blake asked. "You got a better place in mind?"

Jaxi backed against the door until it opened. "No, the barn is fine. You want to arrange a seat by the training pole?"

Blake delivered the rest of the plates to a group of silent men all wearing enormous grins on their faces.

"Someone here got the bad habit of listening at doors?" Blake let his possessive feelings show.

"Holy shit, Blake, you've got to let us come watch," Joel begged.

Blake plopped a plate of pie in front of him. "In. Your. Dreams. I find any one of your scrawny hides near the barn, and I'll convince Dad to let you handle the newborn lambs Christmas Eve all by yourself."

He ignored his own plate of dessert and hightailed it out the door. The boys could clean up—he had a show to attend.

Jaxi slipped through the door into the long hallway. She dropped her bag onto a chair and tugged off her robe.

Blake had turned on the overhead speakers, and the walls strummed with the local country station. She paced to the far end of the barn where the horses' training area was located. In the center of the room, a solid metal post they used for putting foals through their paces rose vertically.

Her heart beat faster as she anticipated Blake's reaction to her dancing. It seemed forever since he'd touched her intimately, and she had no intention of waiting anymore.

He reclined in his chair, relaxed and at ease. Until she noticed his fingers gripped his belt buckle a little too tight. His eyes gone a little too wild.

Perfect.

She took a deliberate stroll behind him. Close enough to drag her fingertips along his shoulders and through the short curls at his neckline. She stepped away to grasp the upright pole cemented in the middle of the room.

And danced.

She started slow and easy, with her hips and torso close to the pole. Her jean shorts rode high on her ass and low on her hips, and showed off the long expanse of leg exposed between the top of her cowboy boots and the shorts. The studded denim vest pressed her breasts until her cleavage threatened to fall out every time she breathed.

She'd picked the outfit deliberately. The girl who had trained her wanted her to wear high heels, and Jaxi learned to dance in them as well, but the boots said it all. She was a country girl through and through, and there was nothing sexier.

She let her head drop back, hanging on to her cowboy hat. She wrapped a leg around the pole while she swung her upper body free, one hand skimming her skin. Over the vest and the buttons, letting a couple loose and exposing more of her body to Blake's vision.

Jaxi pulled off her hat in one smooth motion and let the long hair she'd tucked inside bounce around her shoulders, swinging free. The length stroked her skin, caressing as it fell.

She danced, feeling wicked and sexy and totally in control of her body. The beat of the song echoed in her heart, bounced off the walls and traveled through her limbs to heat her from the inside out. The song finished far too soon. She closed her eyes to focus, breathing hard for a minute before she stepped back from the pole and faced Blake.

He'd opened his jeans and sat stroking himself as he stared at her, raw desire flushing his skin. She watched in fascination as he pulled with firm motions, the length of his cock hard and ready. It had been so long, and she was more than ready to renew the physical part of their relationship.

"Take off your vest."

"Does this mean the wooing is over?"

Blake caught her gaze with his, and the answer flashed heat through her as if she'd stepped in front of a blazing fire on a winter's day.

Oh, yeah.

Jaxi took her time, finally unbuttoning the last snap, and let the garment fall to the ground behind her.

"Holy shit, you've got nipple rings."

"Clip-ons. You like them?"

He growled. Jaxi licked her fingertips, then rolled her nipples. She let the sound of her pleasure flow over him.

"The shorts. Off."

Jaxi moved with deliberate slowness, unsnapping, unzipping, turning her back toward him as she lowered the material over her ass an inch at a time. She wanted to drive Blake mad with want. She startled when his hand touched her skin, hot and moist from touching his cock. He tugged her hips to draw her closer.

"You going to leave those boots on for me, sexy cowgirl?"

"You know it."

Blake stripped down, all hard, glistening muscles, replacing his own boots before standing. He circled her again, like in the kitchen, only this time they were both naked.

Except for their cowboy boots.

Blake stared at her, his gaze eating her up. "Slick, I don't even know where to begin on you. I need to taste those nipples with those pretty little rings. I want to lick your entire body. I want to kiss your sweet lips all night long. But all I can think of right now is finding out how good a cowgirl you are."

Jaxi ran her hand down his chest, playing with the hairs that led to where his cock stood at attention, weeping with need. "You wanna take me for a ride, cowboy?"

Blake swept her into his arms. Jaxi wrapped her legs around his waist, felt his shaft hard against her heated core. He shifted his hands to her ass, and with one quick adjustment, he penetrated her. He was hot and huge, and Jaxi felt every inch as he forged into skin that was tender from too much, too soon, but she didn't want him to stop. The pleasure rose above the faint discomfort as more fluid coated them both, smoothing the thrusts of his body as he drove deeper and deeper. Blake used his strong arms to support her, to weld them together intimately while he stood in the middle of the room. She squeezed him hard, reveled in the heat of his body. The tingle of the breast clips radiated out, upping the sensations slowly driving her higher, increasing the stimulation as he struck her clit on every plunge.

He lifted her suddenly and spun her, nestling her hips back against him. Blake centered himself and pressed in from behind, his hands cupping her breasts, his thumbs and forefingers tugging on the nipple rings while his hips pistoned.

"I need to touch. I need to feel you, all soft and welcoming under my hands. So wet and tight and everything I need. Damn, I need *you.*"

She was going up in flames, all the heat from teasing him at the table, the knowledge she'd turned him on with her dancing, all the love she'd seen in his eyes pulling her closer and closer to the edge. He drew both breasts together into one hand and dropped the other to brush her clitoris and she cried out. Her body squeezed his cock, tried to lock him in place as he continued to rub and thrust.

"Give it to me, Jaxi, don't hold back. I ain't going to stop until you come around me one more time."

Tension drew toward a peak again. She was so wet fluid clung to the inside of her thighs, easing their joining.

"Blake, oh *hell.*" The explosion radiated from her core to the tips of her fingers, every ridge on his cock more pronounced as her sheath clutched tighter around him. Blake cried in triumph, his arms supporting her against his torso as his cock pumped and jerked inside her.

He cradled her close while he shuffled backward, his cock nestled deep within her. He collapsed into the chair, draping her legs over the arms to let him touch where they connected. Jaxi leaned her head on his shoulder and tried to stop the aftershocks from ripping her away from him, still hard between her legs.

One hand cupped her breast. With the other Blake ran a slow finger along the seam between his cock and her pussy, the wickedest sensation ever.

The most intimate touch.

"Damn, that was the sexiest thing I've ever seen."

She couldn't speak. Could barely breathe.

They lay in the chair until Blake softened enough he slid from her body. He twisted her in his arms, both of them sticky with sweat and come, and Jaxi realized she didn't care one bit. She'd never felt more alive.

Blake loosened one of the nipple rings. He pressed his palm against the stinging tip for a minute before removing the other one. Dragging his jeans closer, he reached into a pocket to slip the rings away. He kissed her and cradled her against the beating of his heart.

"Jaxi, I tried to ask you something the other day before the munchkins invaded our picnic."

She sat up a little, glowing from their shared heat.

Blake grinned. He kissed her hand and slipped something cold on her finger.

"It's temporary. We can go pick up something real in Calgary or Edmonton, or even online I guess. I wanted—"

Jaxi kissed him to silence and leaned back to examine the ring. He'd woven two horseshoe nails together, smooth and shiny. It was simple and beautiful and evoked feelings in her she hadn't thought possible to grow any stronger.

He held up his hand to show off a matching ring, and she fought back tears.

"Can we can be ready by October? Ma and Dad got married Thanksgiving weekend, and I figure a wedding would make a real fine reason to be thankful."

Jaxi drew a contented breath and nodded.

He paused for a minute, then gave an embarrassed cough. "You notice we forgot to use something? Again?"

Jaxi blushed. "I was too interested in what we were doing to worry about it."

Blake let out a big breath. "This past week I thought about the fact we've had sex with no protection, a couple times already. I also pondered that lecture you gave me, that first night we made love."

"Lecture?" She shot him her best evil eye.

"Hey, I'm not saying I didn't deserve it. In fact, I earned more of an ass kicking than you gave me that night. It was reckless of me to put you in that position, no matter how right you were about us being together no matter what the outcome. I shouldn't have acted all territorial until we'd talked about the future."

Jaxi wasn't sure where he was going with this. "And the next time? In the kitchen? And now—you're not being territorial now by leaving off a condom?"

"Now I'm totally staking my claim. Like a bloody caveman." He brought their lips together and caught her in mid-laugh. When he finally released her from the kiss it was to back up only a couple of inches. "This time I figured I had your permission—something I didn't have that first night in the cabin. But after you told me very plainly you didn't think us having a baby was a mistake, I thought you might not mind us getting started on a family right quick. I know I wouldn't mind a bit."

The delight in her core turned from a tiny flutter of happiness to a wash of nearly unbearable joy. Having him and a family? "Oh God, Blake."

"Good oh God, or *you're ready to kill me* oh God?"

They were getting married. They could have a baby soon. Wild, incredible, unbelievable. "You're safe, no murder on the agenda. I'm just as responsible for birth control as you are, if it comes to that."

"Just as irresponsible, you mean." His grin flashed bright, and she nodded ruefully. "I also did something this week I'd never done before. I did the math. You know when I was born?"

"May seventeenth."

"Hmm. I've heard that planning for life takes different routes for different folks. But it sure looks like I'm following in my daddy's footsteps in more ways than one."

Oh boy. "You talking six boys?"

"Maybe. Hate to remind you, it's tradition. Great-Grandpa started it."

They dressed and strolled away from the barn hand in hand, Blake playing with the ring on her finger with his thumb.

"So, when are you going to 'fess up and tell me what other classes you've taken? The interesting ones you wouldn't share last week..."

Jaxi raised her gaze to his. "Let's see. Self-defense and boxing."

"Handy for those six boys we're going to have."

"Stop it. Personal massage."

"Nice. What else?" Blake drew her close as he led her back to the cabin. It had been worth the wait to know she was finally his. No more questioning if he'd be able to hold her heart.

She was his. He was hers. It was enough.

Chapter Twenty-Two

Canadian Thanksgiving

"How long do we wait?" Blake plopped down on the edge of the mattress.

Jaxi burrowed a little farther under the covers and groaned. "Oh hell, don't rock the bed."

Blake pulled the edge of the quilt free and smoothed his fingers along her neck, rubbing gently. He leaned over and kissed her nape. "You've got to get up sometime, Slick."

"Go away."

Blake chuckled and drew the blankets back, a tug at a time. She was still warm and soft from sleep, cheeks rosy, and the subtle scent of her skin made his mouth water. He rolled her carefully to her back and smoothed his hands down her body all the way to her toes. He picked up a foot and massaged his thumbs along the bottom length.

"Oh, yeah. You keep that up, and I promise I'll be real nice to you later."

Blake snuck in a nip to her arch. "You're already going to be real nice to me. How long do we have to wait?"

Jaxi opened her eyes with reluctance. "I don't know, read the box. Why do we need that thing anyway?"

"'Cause I want to know for sure."

Jaxi sat and snuggled in close.

"You ready for today, Jaxi?"

"I've been ready for a long time, but..."

He kissed her eyelids, stroked her hair, held her close.

Three more hours and they'd be standing in front of their family and friends, saying the words to join them as a couple. Together and forever and everything that went with it.

It felt so right.

"But what?"

Those big eyes stared at him as she traced a finger along his jaw. Her touch was light but it echoed through his whole body.

"I'm a little scared."

Blake shook his head. "You? Scared? Hell, woman, I've always admired how fearless you were. Even as a little tyke, the first time I saw you, half-naked, covered in mud and whaling on Travis. You were so damn proud you never gave a hint to how much you hurt."

"I was only seven and Travis deserved it. You're never going to let me forget that fight, are you?"

Blake stroked a finger over her lips. "Nope, I like it that you know how to use your fists."

"You like a woman who fights?"

Blake kissed her. "I love a woman who fights. I think I fell in love with you the day I found you taking on that boy who was planning to drown the kittens."

Jaxi's eyes flashed. "You never did let me finish him off. He was ready to go home crying to his mama—"

"Yeah, but he was about three years older than you and a whole lot bigger. Tell me when you knew you wanted me."

Jaxi nuzzled at his neck, her lips brushing his rough stubble. "I fell in love with you when you came to the school for the Professional Day talks. You told everyone all about how the ranch was managed, and the hard work and caring needed to keep the animals happy and everything. I decided right then and there I was going to be the one that helped you."

His jaw dropped. "Jaxi, you must have been about ten years old when I gave that talk."

She flashed him a gorgeous smile. "I told you I've loved you forever."

He cradled her tenderly, enjoying their embrace. There was one last lingering concern he had to share. He had to start this marriage with a clean slate and somehow he'd never managed to bring it up while they were wooing. His chest tightened. "Jaxi, I've got to tell you. Travis and you and me. I mean, there was this one time…"

Jaxi wiggled back, her cheeks slowly flushing with colour. "Oh, shit."

He narrowed his eyes. She looked guilty, but he was sure that was his own emotion reflecting back. "I have to confess the first time you touched me wasn't the night after the pool hall. You kinda… Well, there was this time earlier when you hit on me." He hurried to reassure her. "I mean you were out of it and nothing really happened. I don't think you were aware you were with me." He stuttered to a stop, not sure there was much else he could say.

Her face glowed red but her eyes twinkled with mischief. "Um, Blake, if you're talking about the trip home from the Stampede? I knew it was you."

A funny feeling tickled his stomach. "You knew?" *Holy shit, she'd known all the time?*

She licked at her lips and nodded. "I don't remember much from the start, but suddenly it was like I woke up. Well, I wasn't sure how I'd gotten into the situation, but there was no way in hell I was going to give up the opportunity once I had it."

He stared at her. *Unbelievable.* "You are more trouble than anyone I've ever met in my life."

Blake shook his head, and they both laughed, soft at first and then louder until he was lying flat on his back beside her.

When they finally calmed and he wiped the tears from his eyes, he noticed the time. "Damn, we've got to get ready."

Jaxi stood slowly, biting her lip. Blake swung around and wrapped his arms around her waist, keeping her close as he sat on the bed.

"I'm sure it's done by now," Blake teased.

Jaxi leaned into him as he kissed her belly. "I can't believe you woke me early to pee on a stick. Just remember I already told you the answer."

Blake followed her into the tiny bathroom, crowding against her back. He dropped his chin to her shoulder as she lifted the small white indicator.

"What's it say?" He kissed her neck. Couldn't stop touching her.

"It says you owe me a trip to Calgary to buy maternity clothes like I already told you last week."

Blake slipped his hands over her still flat stomach, imagining how it would feel round and heavy with their baby. All the doubts, all his worries were a thing of the past.

The future was feeling mighty fine.

Jaxi looked at the community people gathered around, faces gleaming at them with delight. Blake's fingers interlocked with hers as he led them firmly down the path toward the outdoor barbecue reception.

"You sure we need to stay for this?" Blake whispered in her ear. "'Cause I got plans."

Jaxi poked him in the side. "We have a whole lot of tomorrows for sex but we're only getting married once. Behave."

Blake grumbled under his breath. "I want to get to the good stuff."

They were swept apart into a sea of well-wishers.

Everywhere Jaxi looked she saw family. Matt and Travis manned the barbecue with Mike, grilling a steady stream of thick steaks. Joel was in charge of the music, and she smiled as he raced to make sure everything was ready at the large dance area they'd built on the lawn. Jesse mixed drinks and flirted with the girls while he restocked the large ice-filled buckets with long-necked beer bottles. Marion, finally free of her cast, visited with Jaxi's parents while Daniel hovered at her side.

Jaxi watched Blake as he spoke with their friends, laughing and receiving congratulations from their neighbours. Her heart filled with joy at the realization she was living her dream.

It wasn't long before they were back together, swaying on the dance floor for a first dance. Jaxi slipped into his arms and sighed with happiness.

"You're looking mighty sexy in them boots, Mrs. Coleman." He twirled her a bit and let her skirt flare against his legs. "You going to tell me if you've got panties under that pretty little dress?"

"Of course, I'm wearing panties." Blake's face fell a little. Jaxi lifted a brow. "You going to pout because I wanted pretty undies to remember this day?"

"You'll have plenty to remember it by without needing some bits of fluff and lace."

She was sure she would, but still.

"Think of it this way. You enjoy unwrapping presents, don't you?" Heat swelled between them, and Blake drew her closer, his fingers splayed possessively over the open keyhole in the back of her dress. She rested her head on Blake's shoulder, dancing close and easy. She waited until he relaxed completely before she spoke again. "Of course, if you don't want to unwrap I made sure nothing would get in your way."

Jaxi counted slowly, aiming for ten. Before she'd reached five, Blake jerked for a moment, and they stumbled. He recovered in time to keep them upright but she'd felt the increase in his heart rate.

"You saying your panties have no crotch? Hot damn, are you trying to kill me right here on the dance floor?" He nudged his erection harder into her body. "Now we have to keep dancing until I can walk past my ma without blushing and embarrassing everyone."

She laughed.

His voice, dark and husky, drifted over her skin like a caress. "There will be a price to pay."

"I love paying my debts. You can strip-search me later."

He stumbled again, and this time the laughter welled up from deep inside her until it burst out and flowed over them both. Swaying on the dance floor, family and friends all around, Jaxi felt the satisfaction she'd been working to achieve for so many years. She'd finally come home, and it wasn't the land or the house or even the family she'd just joined.

It was Blake, and he was all the home she'd ever need.

Bonus Chapter: The Beginning

Lazy Days of Summer, fourteen years earlier

The screams rising from the coulee had changed in the past ten minutes from fun to fearful. Blake flicked the reins to head Midnight over to see which one of his little brothers was in need of getting his britches tanned. Because sure enough when they weren't fighting for each other, they were fighting each other.

Blake let Midnight take her head as she picked her footing down the steep trail that led toward the swimming hole where loud shrieks continued to echo off the clay embankments. Individual voices grew clearer and Blake grinned. It wasn't often Travis ended up on the hurting side of the equation.

He rounded the bend and darted his gaze over the scene. Chaos was in full reign. His youngest four brothers and a spare little boy, all in jean cutoffs and nothing else, were covered from head to toe in dark mud. Joel and Jesse, the six-year-old twins, raced in circles, waving their hands frantically while they shrieked at the top of their lungs. Twelve-year-old Daniel was attempting to pry the skinny newcomer off Travis with one hand, his free hand swatting the air with desperate jerks.

Travis screamed again—the eight-year-old was madder than Blake had ever heard the little bully. His attacker was the only one in the area not hollering or swearing at the top of his lungs. Blake watched as the kid swung and connected another solid blow to Travis's jaw.

Time to stop the fun and games.

"Enough, you little hoodlums." Blake dismounted and waded in, ready to pull the combatants apart and deliver a timely *big brother from hell* speech. "Every one of you, get your..."

Then he realized what was causing all the arm swinging and at least half the swearing. Just to the side of the main fight lay a giant wasp nest.

It appeared to have been ripped clean in two.

Blake felt a little like swearing now himself. "Daniel, get the twins back to the house. Take Midnight, and clean her saddle completely after you get hosed off."

Pausing to make sure Daniel nodded in agreement, he turned his attention to the screaming boys at his feet.

Wasps whizzed around them, and he felt the first sting on his leg. Pulling hard, he lifted the still-swinging blond banshee, grabbed Travis by the wrist and toppled the three of them into the shallows of the swimming hole. "Get ready to hold your breath. Travis, I mean it. Stop screaming and take a big breath. On the count of three."

He pulled them all under, pushed off the bottom toward the middle of the stream and allowed the gentle current to float them for a good ten count before letting their heads pop up to the surface of the water. The angry buzz was still audible but fading as he hauled his squirming cargo to the shore, dragging the boys over the grassy bottom to the lower edge of the trail.

"Get on up there. Now! Get home and let Ma deal with you. Little idiots, what were you thinking?"

Travis knew enough to sense Blake's patience was gone. He turned and raced up the hill without even complaining that it was someone else's fault. The other kid. He didn't seem to know it was time to stop fighting and start running.

"You ain't my boss." Eyes narrowed, chin jutting out as he glared up at Blake. It would have been funny if they both weren't dripping wet and filthy.

"I am now, Slick. Get on up there. My ma will see to those welts before we get you home. Unless you'd prefer I take you home now and let your folks deal with you?"

The skinny little thing didn't look more than five years old. Pale wisps of hair stuck up where the mud had washed off, but the dirt seemed permanent on other portions of the creature. "They ain't there. My mom's gone to town for grub. I can take care of myself."

Blake counted to ten. There was no way he could go home and tell his mom he'd let some little tyke wander off without his folks—wasp-stung, filthy, and pounded from fighting Travis.

Even though it looked like the little beast had gotten the better of that particular deal.

"What's your name, kid?"

"Jax."

"Jack?"

He was given the you're-too-stupid-for-words look. "J-A-X. My name is Jackson, but Momma and Daddy call me Jax."

"Well, Jax, you gotta come home with me for a bit. If your folks are gone, you could probably use a little dinner. We'll hose off the mud and get something to eat. I think my ma's got leftover chicken around we could nab. Deal?"

Blake knew the second he mentioned food that it would work. The kid was skinny as all get out. Jax scrambled up the embankment and trotted next to him, little legs working double time to keep up with Blake's wide stride.

At seventeen Blake was getting into his full growth. He was tall enough already that this little guy seemed awfully short.

"How old are you, Jax?"

"Seven."

That was surprising. Jax couldn't be any bigger than the twins.

"I've never seen you around before. Did you just move in?"

"The blue trailer on the edge of the road. Ma said it's a dump, but I think it's okay." Typical kid, he kept stopping to check out the grasshoppers and spiders that scurried off the trail as they quickstepped toward the house.

Must be the new renters that he'd overheard his parents talking about. The dad had signed on with one of the local hauling companies. Hard work. Jax's dad would be gone for days at a time. Blake took another look at the kid. His little face and arms were covered with swelling welts, but he hadn't made a noise of complaint about them.

"So you wanna tell me what happened down at the swimming hole?"

Jax looked up at him in surprise. "I ain't one of your brothers. You gonna let them tell you what happened, right?"

Blake frowned. "I figure you can tell me just fine. You won't lie to me, will you?"

Jax stopped dead. "Lying is for babies and cheats. I ain't no baby and I ain't no cheat."

"So, tell me. What happened?"

"Me and Joel and Jesse were swimming and playing a game and Travis came and said he'd make me eat a frog. So I told him that frogs were a deli-cat-zee and only the really important people could eat them so I thought that was a really fine thing.

"Then he said I had a stick up my butt and he was going to teach me a thing or two. So I said he was too stupid to teach me anything. Then Joel tried to tell him something and Travis pushed him into the mud. Of course Jesse tried to help Joel and Travis pushed him down too. Then Daniel started yelling at Travis and Travis said some bad words and then he tried to push Daniel into the mud and Joel and Jesse were trying to jump on Travis and then…"

Blake stared in amazement. Usually when he asked his brothers what happened he got "he looked at me funny so I hit him" as an answer. Not a five-minute nonstop detailed play-by-play.

They'd reached the house, and there was no sign of any of the rest of the culprits except for a pile of filthy wet shorts lumped by the still-running hose. Blake pointed Jax toward the pile.

"…well, I slipped and fell in the mud and I thought maybe that could be the end and we'd just play for a while. You know, we were all dirty, so why not, but Travis came over and pinched me…"

Yeah, that was Travis. He fought dirty.

Blake stripped off his wet things and turned the hose on himself. Ma put up with a lot, having six boys around the house, but he knew better than to enter the house covered in river water and mud. Even if he went through the basement door straight into a shower.

"…but when I climbed the tree he called me a coward." Jax finally stopped talking and put his hands on his hips. "I ain't no coward. So when I spotted the nest I thought it would be a good idea and—"

"Jax. Talk while you take off your stuff. I'll hose you down."

"Oh. Okay. So I pulled off the nest but I kinda fell and when I landed I must have made a funny noise because Travis called me a 'pig in the wallow' and it made me really mad so I walked up to him and told him at least I wasn't an ass without a barn and then I pulled that nest apart and things kinda just happened after that."

The shorts dropped quick like and Jax turned in the spray to let Blake rinse off his back. Welts rose everywhere, and Blake turned down the pressure on the hose. It had to hurt like the blazes.

Then the kid turned around and Blake noticed for the first time what he probably should have figured out sooner.

Jax was a girl.

About the Author

Vivian Arend has hiked, biked, skied and paddled her way around most of North America and parts of Europe. Throughout all the wandering in the wilderness, stories have been planted and they are bursting out in vivid colour. Paranormal, twisted fairytales, red-hot contemporaries—the genres are all over.

Between times of living with no running water, she home schools her teenaged children and tries to keep up with her husband—the instigator of most of the wilderness adventures.

She loves to hear from readers: vivarend@gmail.com. You can also drop by www.vivianarend.com for more information on what is coming next.

She wants it. He's got it...and a whole lot more.

Turn It Up
© *2011 Vivian Arend*
The Turner Twins, Book 2

Maxwell Turner considers his stubborn and resourceful attitude a plus. After all, it usually gets him what he wants—except for Natasha Bellingham. The long-time family friend may be ten years older than he, but so what? He's plenty old enough to know they belong together. Now all he has to do is convince her.

Over the past few years Natasha's love life has degenerated into a series of bad clichés. Her biological clock is ticking—loudly. As a proven architect with her own house-design company, she's financially ready for a baby. Who says she needs a permanent man in her life for that? She just needs a "donation".

When Max discovers Natasha's future plans include artificial insemination, he's outraged. She wants to get pregnant? No problem. He's more than willing to volunteer—no turkey basters involved.

But there's one non-negotiable clause: He wants forever. And he intends to do everything in his power—fair and unfair—to make it happen.

Warning: This title contains one younger man ready, aimed and hell bent on giving one woman everything she wants. Includes interludes against the wall, in a Jacuzzi, on a car hood and even—shockingly enough—on a bed or two. Oh, and about that porch swing? Yup...

Available now in ebook and print from Samhain Publishing.

Good girls can play rough too...

Cowgirls Don't Cry
© *2010 Lorelei James*
Rough Riders, Book 10

Jessie McKay has accepted her marriage to Luke McKay wasn't perfect. After two years of widowhood, she's ready to kick up her bootheels—until Luke's younger brother shows up to spoil her fun. But if Brandt thinks she'll ever take orders from another McKay male, he's got manure for brains.

Brandt McKay has avoided his sweet, sexy sister-in-law ever since the night he confessed his feelings for her weren't the brotherly type. Unexpectedly faced with proof of Luke's infidelity, Brandt is forced to ask for Jessie's help in taking care of Luke's young son. Jessie agrees on one condition—she wants Brandt's boots exclusively under her bed for the duration.

The sexual heat that's always simmered between them ignites. Brandt is determined to make the temporary situation permanent, proving to Jessie he's a one-woman man. And Jessie is shaken by feelings she's sworn never to have again for any man...especially not a McKay.

Warning: Contains branding-iron-hot sex, the one McKay on earth who wants to be tamed, and a woman who's decided tame is for nice girls who finish last.

Available now in ebook and print from Samhain Publishing.

He opened his home. She stole his heart...and his money.

Trespass
© 2011 Meg Maguire

Many would envy veterinarian Russ Gray's life in rural Montana's wide-open spaces. Russ calls it lonely. In a country with more cattle than eligible females, he doesn't envision his seven years as a widower ending anytime soon. Until a mysterious woman lands at his door in the dead of night, riddled with buckshot.

Sarah Novak hates lying to such a kind, handsome man, but if an upstanding citizen like Russ finds out why she's been three weeks on the run, he'd surely turn her in. Yet she can't refuse his offer to let her stay until she heals, no questions asked.

From the start they fall into an easy companionship, then teasing flirtation flares into an unexpected intimate connection. But no matter how right it feels in his arms, guilt tugs at Sarah's heart. Russ doesn't deserve what she must do next.

When Russ wakes up with an empty bed—and an empty wallet—his first instinct isn't to call the cops...it's to catch her and find out why his urge to protect her overshadows all reason. Because he's had a taste of real passion, and he's not letting it slip away without a fight.

Available now in ebook and print from Samhain Publishing.

PUBLISHING

It's all about the story...

HORROR

www.samhainpublishing.com

CPSIA information can be obtained at www.ICGtesting.com
Printed in the USA
BVOW031016181012

303359BV00001B/75/P

9 781609 287993